Praise for
The Flex of the Thumb:

"Vano is the greatest comic character since Inspector Clouseau."
- *Dr. Donald Raycraft, Chilton Productions*

"Every kid has dreamed, at one time or another, of being able to pitch like Vano Lucas. I loved the hell out of the book."
- *Denny Matthews, Announcer, Kansas City Royals*

"This book is hysterical. I only wish we could publish it. I expect it to be a cult classic on college campuses."
-*Regina Griffin, Vice President, Editor-in-Chief, Holiday House*

JAMES W.
BENNETT

THE
FLEX
OF THE
THUMB

Pin Oak Press

The Flex of the Thumb
by
James W. Bennett

PUBLISHER'S NOTE:
This is a work of fiction. Names, characters, places, and incidents are products of the author's imagination, or are used fictitiously. Any resemblance to actual occurrences or actual people, living or dead, is entirely coincidental.

Copyright © 1996 James W. Bennett
Cover Art by Sue Krumrei
Printed in the U.S.A.

All rights reserved. No part of this book may be reproduced or transmitted in any form or by any means (electronic, mechanical, photocopying, recording, or any other) without express written consent of the author and the publisher, except for the inclusion of brief quotations in reviews.

Publisher's Cataloging-in-Publication Data
Bennett, James W.
The Flex of the Thumb
I. Title
Library of Congress Catalog Card Number
    96-67509
ISBN 0-9651030-8-0

Published By:

Pin Oak Press
P.O. Box 9169
Springfield, IL 62791

Please address all inquiries to the address above.

This book is dedicated
to the memory of Chad Lobdell,
an author dying much too young.

Chapter One

Looking back, it was clear how there were foreshadowing vibes even before there was ever a telling blow to the head. They weren't the deep, chambered, transforming kind, nor were they long in duration, but they were there all the same. Nothing comes from nothing, in other words, certainly not the ever-widening circle of particular waves which serves to define the nature of the cosmos. What confluence of forces it was that framed a window on the universe along the inscape of Vano's psyche? Who can say about these things?

But Vano had vibes, for instance, the day of the senior class field trip to the Magic Mountain amusement park near Santa Clarita. A girl fell to her death from the Sky Chute. A few nearby onlookers were demonstrably shocked and traumatized, but park activities went right ahead with business as usual. Nothing missed a beat, or so it seemed to Vano. He felt resonant vibes from outside and from within, timbreing up from some deep and private, cthonic place. The sky seemed to shimmer with an orange hue.

Vano recovered within a few moments, and was able to go about his business. That business included swilling down as much of Treece's smuggled beer as possible, and finding a private place in the picnic grove for planking Ann-Marie Pillsbury, who had been hanging on him all day.

There was also the time when Vano stood on the

mound of the San Bernardino High School baseball field toeing the rubber. In the beginning, it was only a low ringing in his ears. And not precisely a ringing either, but more of a resonance like a tuning fork struck in a very low register, crescendoing before slowly dissipating. He turned away from his catcher long enough to stare up at the puffy California clouds floating slowly across their blue sky backdrop.

As always, the crowd assembled to watch Vano pitch was overflow. The permanent bleachers were full, as well as a section of temporary seats. Two thousand people or so, standing, lined both foul lines and even filled in behind the outfield fence. The best seats, those directly behind home plate, were occupied by major league scouts who cradled their speed guns and charted Vano's pitches.

Felix Gomez, the Apple Valley catcher, approached the mound. "What's the matter, Man? One more batter, okay?" As he spoke, he adjusted the sponges he used to reinforce his catcher's mitt whenever Vano pitched.

"It's the ringing," Vano told him.

"Not the ringing, Man. Just one more batter."

"Don't worry, it's over now."

The relieved Gomez said, "Good. We've got a two-hour bus ride when the game is over. After that, I've got a date with Becky. I think I might get to hide the weinie, okay?"

"You wish," said Vano, shaking his head. "It was just an episode; I'm okay now." He glanced at the final out, an undersized freshman with lots of pimples by the name of Scottie Wiggins, sent up to bat against his will. "Let's just get the goddam game over with. I think I'll throw this little shit a couple sliders."

"Oh Jesus Christ, what the hell for?"

Vano was grinning with a malevolent gleam in his

eye. "Maybe we can get him to load his pants; whatta you think?"

"I told you what I think. Let's just get the game over. You've struck out every batter with the fast ball, we don't need to goof on this kid."

"Not every batter. One guy grounded out to first."

"You knocked the bat out of his hands," Gomez reminded Vano. "What can I say?"

By this time the home plate umpire was at the mound and out of patience. "What's the problem, boys?"

Gomez turned to the ump. "He wants to throw his fuckin' slider."

"You watch your mouth with me," said the umpire, whose name was Culpepper.

"He wants to throw his freakin' slider."

"That's better. So what's the problem?"

"I can't catch his slider," explained Gomez. "He throws it 98 miles an hour and it's got about a 15-inch bite. I can't catch it even if it's in the strike zone."

Briefly, Culpepper tried to imagine what a 98-mile-an-hour pitch could do to various parts of his anatomy if the catcher missed the ball. He said to Vano, "No sliders, kid. Now can we get on with it?"

It didn't occur to Vano that by dictating pitches, the umpire was exceeding his authority. He said, "Okay, what the hell; let's get the goddam game over with."

Gomez pulled down his mask as he crouched low behind home plate. He gave Vano the sign, just the index finger, but wondered for the umpteenth time why he bothered giving signs at all. *Was it a requirement?* The umpire got down low behind him. The batter, Scottie Wiggins, stood as far from the plate as the rules allowed, and then some. With his eyes tightly closed, he rested the bat on his right shoulder.

Vano went into his wind-up.

The pitch was a blur with a 15-inch tail that exploded up and in over the inside corner. Into Gomez' mitt like a rifle shot.

Umpire Culpepper called strike one. "How do you catch that thing?" he asked Gomez.

"I don't really catch it, he just hits the mitt. It's sort of like catchin' a foul tip. Mostly luck."

"Jesus Christ."

In the bleachers behind the screen, Vano's father, Vernon, made a quick survey of the speed guns in his vicinity. They did not all register exactly the same. Some of them tracked the pitch at 112 miles per hour, while others had readings as high as 115. Vernon Lucas smiled. He dreamed of stocks and bonds, real estate holdings, and maybe even a modest island in the Carribean.

Vano threw two more fast balls, same location, same velocity. The ump punched out the relieved Scottie Wiggins, who trailed his bat toward the dugout. The tell-tale moisture which darkened the inseams of his uniform trousers didn't matter; he would live to tell about this day.

Lying in the grass and chewing clover stems, the outfielders had to be told by the shortstop that the game was over. Vano left the mound and started shaking hands amidst a throng of well-wishers and back-slappers. It was another perfect game. He had faced the minimum, 21 batters, striking out 20. He never did get to throw his slider.

In the parking lot, Ann-Marie honked and waved from behind the wheel of her yellow Geo convertible. Vano said to Gomez, "We'll ride back with Ann-Marie. Go get Becky."

"If we don't ride the bus we're breakin' team rules."

"Tell me."

"We could get suspended," Gomez reminded him.

"We could even get kicked off."

Vano's reply was a scornful one: "They're going to kick me off the team? Listen to it, Gomez."

"Okay, but what about me?"

"They're gonna kick my catcher off? I don't think so. Go get Becky. Or, you can wuss out and ride the bus. It's no skin off my ass one way or the other."

Gomez rode in the back seat with Becky. Vano slid behind the wheel. "Move over," he said to Ann-Marie. Vano decided to drive roundabout by way of Grass Valley Road, along the rugged terrain which surrounded Miller Canyon. It was the long way north to be sure, but nobody seemed to notice. Ann-Marie was too busy explaining the financial aid package offered her by the Victorville Beauty Academy, while Gomez was locked onto his back seat schmoozing with Becky.

Somewhere between Twin Peaks and the merger with highway 173, Vano pulled off the snaking road at a deserted sidebar. "Why are we stopping?" Ann-Marie asked him.

"Just follow me, everything's cool." Taking her by the hand, he led her around a large boulder configuration in the direction of a clearing in amongst some dense chapparal. When they were alone, he began untying the strings which secured her pink halter top.

She offered some resistance, at first. "What are you doing, Vano?"

"Duh. Let's try twenty questions."

"But I was trying to tell you about my financial aid package. Aren't you interested?"

"Is that what it was?"

"But don't you want to hear about it?"

"Ann-Marie, it's time to cut to the chase. What do you think this is about?"

Her breasts loosed in the high desert breeze, Ann-Marie folded her arms across her chest. *Wasn't it demeaning to be treated this way? Wasn't Vano Lucas an arrogant bastard to assume that she was his for the taking?*

"What about Gomez and Becky?"

"They'll take care of themselves," Vano assured her. By this time, he was unzipping his fly. "Take your shorts off, Ann-Marie; it's time to get it on."

Ann-Marie had second thoughts about her second thoughts. If she wasn't certain what the self-esteem factor in this equation was, there was one thing she did understand: life as the wife of Vano Lucas, soon to become a multimillionaire, would be immensely preferable to life as a checker at the Red Fox supermarket, her current position, or as a hairstylist/manicurist, which was her likely future position.

With tears forming in her eyes, she nevertheless began removing her pink shorts.

*

In the kitchen of the spacious Lucas condominium, the southern exposure opened on a vast and scenic mountain overlook. While Sister Cecilia, the housekeeper, prepared Vano's breakfast of sausage, eggs, waffles, and toast, she sorted the mail. It was already mid-morning. She asked Vano if he had any plans for the day.

"SSDD," was Vano's answer.

"What do you mean by that, Vano?"

"Same shit, different day."

"Please don't use blasphemy," said Sister Cecilia, who was saved and sanctified.

Vano ignored the rebuke. For all he cared,

blasphemy was some kind of off-speed breaking ball or circle change.

Sister Cecilia gave Vano a flier of coupons from Domino's Pizza. The rest of his mail she comandeered. There were 21 letters addressed to him, from professional teams, colleges and universities, newspapers, magazines, radio stations, and television networks. She took all of them to his father's den where she secured them in a desk drawer. From the den came the sound of the phone tweeting and the answering machine kicking in.

Vano ate his breakfast while Sister ironed her Salvation Army blazer. She worked the iron deftly between the brass buttons. With his mouth full, Vano complained that his life was boring. He said, "The old man won't even let me pitch in one of the summer leagues."

"We've been through this before; he's only trying to do what's best for your future. And please don't call him *the old man*. It's disrespectful."

"My FATHer then. Is that better?"

"Much better."

"My FATHer, my FATHer. It's almost a month since I graduated, and all I get to do is run laps and work out in the weight room."

"Why don't you play some catch with Gomez?"

"I probably will, after supper. That's some cool shit for sure."

"Vano, I asked you nicely about the blasphemy. Maybe when your father gets back from his business trip, you can ask him again about pitching summer baseball."

"Why? So he can shoot me down again?"

"I know it's hard," she consoled. Wearing the blazer, she inspected her appearance in front of the sideboard mirror. She suggested, "Maybe you could get involved in some volunteer activities."

"Right. I think I'll run right down to the V.A. hospital so I can empty some bedpans." He looked at Sister Cecilia, now lifting her chest to smooth the wool lapels. He wondered what she might look like if she lost 10 or 20 pounds and didn't wear such severe clothing. He wondered if she ever got horny or did her religion neutralize urges like that.

Sister ignored his sarcasm and hung the blazer away in the hall closet. She told Vano, "I've been cleaning out the attic. I found some old scrapbooks with lots of pictures of your mother. Would you like to see them?"

Scrapbooks? But he couldn't think of anything better to do. "Sure. Why not?"

She took Vano to the dark attic, where he immediately smacked his head on an exposed beam. Rubbing his head and swearing, he tried to ignore Sister's protestations re his language. They began their examination of the photographs by looking at a shoebox full of snapshots of Vano's mother, in no particular order. School pictures, some of her working in the garden, even a few candids from the wedding reception. They were odds and ends which Vano found mostly boring.

But then there was the scrapbook with the paisley cover. There were some 20 pages or so of pictures which showed Vano's mother with a lot of hairy, bearded people in hippy garb. The gathering place seemed to be a camp or conference center.

Vano looked slowly at the scrapbook photos a second time, when suddenly the vibrations were upon him. *Did they come from the blow on the head?* Sister Cecilia was offering her interpretation: "I think these pictures go back to the sixties."

Vano spoke through the resonance: "Do you remember the sixties?"

"A little bit," answered Sister. "I graduated high school in '72. It was a time of protest. It was called peace and love, but I'm afraid it was mostly all about drugs and immorality."

Vano couldn't hear all of what she said because the vibes were too strong. The two of them were now looking at a series of pictures of Vano's mother sitting beside a guy who looked like a holy man. He had flowing gray hair of shoulder length, and a pointed salt and pepper beard. His linen tunic had a squared neckline and plenty of beadwork.

Vano's vibes were like a reverberating gong. "Who is this person," he asked, "who looks like a prophet?"

"There's no need to yell, Vano, not when I'm sitting right beside you." Having lodged this mild complaint, Sister Cecilia attempted an answer to his question: "I don't know who he is. He looks like a holy man, but the Bible teaches us to beware of the wolf in sheep's clothing. He might have been some kind of occult guru. We can only hope and pray that he was a follower of Our Lord."

Vano heard very little of this. The resonance was too firm and not inclined to abate.

The next thing he knew, he found himself behind the wheel of the Pulsar, his graduation present. Northeast on Highway 15, through a late-lifting fog and dissipating rings of resonance. He was on the way, though he may not have known it consciously, to Entrada College, a small institution of no reputation.

The outdated baseball field at Entrada was in a condition of deterioration, and so was the coach, Rip Radulski. Vano sat on the dugout apron with Radulski, whose rheumy eyes bore witness to his drinking history.

There were eight Entrada players shagging outfield balls and taking infield grounders in the hot sun. The school year was over and so was their season; they were merely working out on their own for summer league play.

"Did I know you were coming for a visit?" Radulski asked.

"Even I didn't know," said Vano. "I just had this sudden urge. Sometimes I get these vibes that I can't understand."

Radulski, who was thoroughly familiar with Vano's talent, said, "If I'da known you were coming, I could've made arrangements for the right kind of visit." What he had in mind was the Garibaldi twins, who had tits out to here and a singular enthusiasm for *menage a trois*.

Vano said, "You're talking about an official visit, like an NCAA thing. I've never had one of those."

"You haven't made any campus visits at all?"

"Nope, none."

Radulski shook his head. "How many schools have contacted you?"

"I'm not sure. I think it's up in the hundreds. My old man screens all the college stuff. Sometimes lately I think about my mother; that's what happened today. My mother went to college here."

"Entrada is your mother's *alma mater?*"

"I wouldn't know about that, all I know is she graduated here."

In his imagination, Radulski suddenly cradled a vision of his baseball team with Vano Lucas perched on the mound. This piece of imagery left him short of breath and very thirsty. "I'm going to need a snort about now," he informed Vano. "Excuse me."

"That's okay."

Radulski took a long, gurgling pull from a pint of Jim Beam. Then he asked, "Is anybody here with you?"

"I'm by myself. If my old man knew I was here he'd probably come unglued."

"Your father doesn't know you're here?"

"Nah. He's in Houston on some kind of business. He always tells me not to waste my time thinkin' about college. I'll probably get a signing bonus between ten and twenty million before the summer's over, so I guess I can see his point. I think school's real boring, anyway. I hate homework."

Even though Coach Radulski could see Vano's father's point too, he had had that glimpse in his mind's eye. He couldn't resist some small gesture which might be in his own best interest: "You don't want to overlook the value of a college education, though. It makes you a well-rounded person."

"Oh yeah?"

"That's what they say. I could show you around the campus if you want. It's pretty small, so it wouldn't take long."

"Nah, that's okay," Vano told him. He was already growing weary of being here, now that the vibes were long gone. He looked out across the tacky, neglected playing field where the craters of stony turf were surrounded by tufts of lambsquarters, buckhorn, and other broadleaf weeds. He could imagine the measly crowds that probably showed up for Entrada home games.

After Radulski finished another modest snort, he screwed the cap back on his bottle. "Would you like to throw a few?"

"I don't think so. I didn't bring any shoes or anything. I just got this urge to drive up here all of a sudden. I get these like vibes sometimes."

"You said that once. But it would be easy for me to get some equipment out of the gym."

"No thanks. I guess I'm out of here."

"I'll be in touch," said Radulski. "I'll call you."

"Don't bother. Every phone call goes through my old man's answering machine." Then Vano drove back home.

*

Reggie Rose was president of Entrada College. Since he had held this position a little less than one year, he was still largely unclear about the duties of a college CEO.

Reggie was anal-retentive in the extreme when it came to his disposition; he liked his things well dusted and systematically placed. He owned a large range of state-of-the-art electronic pleasure gadgetry. He owned a high-tech IBM computer, a Sony VCR, and a great deal of digital stereo equipment which could be operated comfortably by a remote unit. His video tapes, CDs, and computer programs were alphabetized in custom-made oak racks.

He kept all his goodies dust free with his own feather duster. Fastidiousness was a way of life for Reggie Rose, who could spend an entire day cleaning tapes and records, dusting his mouse pad, labeling, and filing. He shampooed his dark brown hair daily, and wore it parted straight down the center of his scalp. His eyeglasses had hexagonal lenses and wire earpieces.

He had never been married, but there were two women in his life. The first was his secretary, Mrs. Askew. Reggie Rose did not like her; he found her officious. The second was his housekeeper, Bertie Kerfoot. She was a slob, and if there was one thing President Rose could not abide, it was a slob.

On this particular morning, Reggie had to deal with the disagreeable elements of both of these women.

He came down to the kitchen for breakfast.

Bertie Kerfoot was a terrible cook. For breakfast, she served him six stale Ritz crackers on a plate with a sprig of dead parsley, and a warm bottle of Dr. Pepper. While he munched dispiritedly, Bertie leaned against the kitchen counter, smoked a cigarette and stared at him.

"These crackers are pretty stale," President Rose observed.

"We need to finish them off before they get *real* stale," responded Bertie Kerfoot. "There's plenty left if you want more."

Reggie declined. Then he complained that this was not a very good breakfast. Bertie said what she always said: "What do you expect from me? Perfect?"

This cavalier attitude toward cuisine was particularly repulsive to Reggie. He cherished good food. He loved to entertain friends at the finest restaurants in town. Sometimes, he liked to cook along with Julia Childs. Reggie could prepare steak *au poivre, cassoulet,* and beef*bourginon.*

Whenever Bertie cooked for him, she usually prepared milk toast, dried beef gravy on Saltine crackers, a can of Chef Boyardee Spaghetti-os, frozen pizza rolls, or Spam *lite.*

While Reggie munched on his powdery Ritz cracker, his mind stubbornly tracked itself into the despondency of returning home late in the evenings from tedious meetings. He liked to relax in his den by turning on the late news. But just as soon as he did, here would come Bertie, shuffling in to join him. She always wore an old faded housecoat which kept falling open, and a hairnet; she had a can of Budweiser in one hand and a cigarette dangling from her lips. It wasn't pretty.

Then she would collapse on the couch. Her cigarette

ash fell on the carpet, she belched repeatedly, she smacked her lips a lot. Loud. Then, after her custom, she would begin nagging Reggie to change channels so she could watch *A Current Affair.*

It was all ruinous to the tranquility of the late news, so Reggie rarely stayed up until the conclusion of the program. He would have given Bertie notice, but she went with the house. The house was furnished for the president, but so was the housekeeper.

Sometimes Reggie Rose dreamed that Bertie Kerfoot might drown in the bathtub, and then he could hire Mary Thorne to come and live with him and be his housekeeper. If he thought about this idea for very long, Reggie became very enthusiastic. Mary Thorne was indeed a *munchkin.*

"Or maybe it's a *liebchen,*" Reggie said aloud. "Maybe that's the word I want."

"Are you speaking to me?" asked Bertie Kerfoot, with smoke streaming from her nostrils. Bertie was very skilled at smoking a cigarette all the way down without once removing it from her lips.

"Never mind," said Reggie. He pushed away from the breakfast table and headed for the office.

Where the officious Mrs. Askew confronted him. She told him that the college was in desperate straits. It was, in fact, about to go under.

"Oh yeah?" challenged Reggie Rose. "Says who?"

"Says the board of trustees," answered Mrs. Askew quickly. She dropped a thick book on his desk. "Here is their report."

Reggie looked at the report. It was bound in a dark blue, semi-hard cover. He decided that it looked real boring and would not be any fun to read.

It would be fun deciding where to *place* it, however. He glanced around his opulent office. There were leather-bound books in floor-to-ceiling bookcases. He had a beautiful walnut desk and a slate coffee table. On the wall facing his desk, an expensive wood carving with letters in high relief spelled out the only principle of administrative leadership which Reggie Rose understood:

TO LEAD IS TO DELEGATE

Reggie decided the slate coffee table would be the best permanent home for the trustees' report.

"You want me to summarize the report for you?" asked Mrs. Askew crisply.

"Why don't you go ahead and do that? I sure wouldn't want to read it."

Mrs. Askew was accustomed to this. Putting on her glasses, she began reading from her notepad: "The college's financial picture is very bleak. Endowments are exhausted, and no new revenues are being generated. Interest on investments is used up. Costs are being met from the principal. The General Revenue fund is depleted. If the college doesn't generate substantial new sources of revenue within the calendar year, we will have no choice but to close our doors."

"This sounds real serious," Reggie had to admit. He slumped in his chair. If the school had to close down, then he would be out of a job. If that was so, he would have no income. He had a Mercedes-Benz, a Trinitron big-screen television set, a 30-foot boat, and an annual membership in an exclusive Palm Springs country club. It took money to have such things.

"There's more," said Mrs. Askew.

"There's more?"

Mrs. Askew continued by pointing out, "The college is scheduled to lose its accreditation. The Western

Association will not renew our accreditation unless certain aspects of our operation are improved immediately."

These observations provoked Reggie into a feisty mode: "Such as? What's wrong with this college, I'd like to know."

"Such as the physical facilities, the curriculum, and the faculty."

"And what's wrong with them?"

"The physical facilities are overcrowded and outdated," informed Mrs. Askew. "The curriculum is archaic and limited. The faculty is undistinguished." She took off her glasses, looked up from her notepad, and said, "In a word, we are just about kaput."

"Kaput?"

"Kaput. Done for. Out of time."

Reggie slumped back in his chair again. This really was very serious and discouraging. He wished Mrs. Askew would leave now, but she simply sat there staring at him expectantly, wagging her crossed leg and popping her gum. Her glasses had rhinestones in the frames. But she didn't seem inclined to leave. Reggie finally said meekly, "What are we going to do?"

"Well, we can't do much of anything without money, can we?"

"Yes, that's so. The money is important, very important. How can we get some?"

Mrs. Askew sat up straighter; she was now enjoying this conversation a great deal. She had a healthy appetite for power, and this was power. She said, "Fund raising is a complex and difficult procedure which takes time, energy, and resourcefulness. Financial resources such as endowment have to be carefully cultivated and nurtured over time. It takes individual giving, public monies, and corporate gifts to build the financial undergirding needed to sustain an institution of higher learning."

Hearing this, Reggie was even more discouraged. "That sure sounds like a lot of work," he said with a pout.

"It is a lot of work," the secretary confirmed. "A great deal of work."

President Rose was glum. This was very serious stuff. The college was indeed in a desperate position. Then he asked, "Did the trustees say anything in their report about our mainframe computer? That's the gem of my leadership. Did they see fit to mention that?"

"Nary a word," replied Mrs. Askew. She followed this terse observation by informing him that a man was waiting to see him.

His visitor turned out to be Rip Radulski, baseball coach. As soon as Radulski introduced himself, Reggie said, "Baseball coach? Where?"

"Right here," answered Radulski. "Here at Entrada."

"You mean our college has a baseball team?"

"Of course," said Radulski, suddenly uneasy. He was here to lobby for funding to rehabilitate the baseball field, but it was plain there was a great deal of groundwork to be laid.

Reggie stood up from his chair in order to stand near his coffee table. He folded his arms across his chest and studied the windblown face of Rip Radulski, stippled with reddish blotches and purplish textures. Plenty of razor nicks. After Reggie assumed a pensive visage, from the corner of his eye he spied the trustees' report. "Please excuse me for just a moment," he said to the baseball coach.

He walked briskly to Mrs. Askew's office. "Tell me something," he said. "Is there anything in the trustees' report about the baseball team?"

"Nary a word," replied Mrs. Askew, without

looking up from her keyboard.

Reggie went back to Radulski. "There's not a word in the trustees' report about the baseball team," he said.

"That's a disgrace, then," said Radulski. "A California college is not supposed to have a baseball team that's ignored."

President Rose, who had grown up in Vermont, found this to be a perplexing remark.

Radulski went on to say he needed funds to bring the Entrada baseball faciltiy up to snuff. "What does up to snuff mean?" Reggie asked him.

"We need to have the field reworked and resodded. The stadium needs to be sandblasted, and we need new bleachers built along the left field line. It would give us more seating and more symmetry."

The idea of more symmetry was always appealing to Reggie Rose, wherever he found it. But he said to Radulski, "Is our current seating capacity inadequate?"

Radulski hesitated. Under normal circumstances, he would not have been reluctant to tell a lie, but these were not normal circumstances. For the first thing, he was stone cold sober, and for the second, this was the college president. On the other hand, telling the whole truth about Entrada baseball crowds would sabotage his cause. He said, "It will be, if Vano Lucas comes to Entrada."

"Who?"

"Vano Lucas."

Reggie wondered if this was a name with which he should be familiar. He decided to take a risk: "And who is Vano Lucas, if I may be so bold?"

"He's the greatest pitcher alive. He's Bob Feller and Sandy Koufax and Nolan Ryan rolled into one."

Reggie wondered who these people were. He said, "How much money are we talking about for this stadium upgrading?"

"Not much," answered Radulski. "Maybe two or three million."

"Two or three million??" Reggie stood up immediately to begin pacing. He pounded his right fist into his left palm, several times. He said to Radulski, "Are you at all familiar with the trustees' report? Do you realize the economic crisis Entrada College is facing?"

Rip Radulski was uncomfortable wearing this suit and tie. He had not taken a drink in nearly 24 hours. He followed a sudden inspiration by saying, "Actually, you could think of the two million as seed money."

Still pacing and pounding his palm, Reggie said, "Seed money?"

"Right. If Vano Lucas comes, we can sell at least ten thousand seats for every home game. At least the games he pitches. That's even after we inflate the ticket prices. Not to mention the big-time guarantees we could get for every game on the road."

Reggie didn't know baseball pitchers from the breeding habits of sea anemones, but this sounded like revenue. It got his attention. "Go on," he said to the coach.

The trace of enthusiasm in Reggie's tone gave Radulski added confidence. He continued, "And that's just the tip of the iceberg. That's the pocket change. If Vano Lucas pitches for us, we'll be on national TV. Not only cable networks like SportsChannel and ESPN, but even regular networks like CBS."

President Rose resumed his seat. His interest was peaking because this coach was talking about lots of national exposure and lots of money. He said, "And this fellow, this what's his name?"

"Vano Lucas."

"This Vano Lucas wants to come to Entrada?"

"I'll put it to you this way," answered Radulski. "Entrada is the only college he's visited. We happen to be his mother's *alma mater*. He hasn't even visited UCLA or Southern Cal, and he doesn't plan to. I'll let you draw your own conclusions." Delivering this lobbying effort without the telling of even one outright lie gave the coach a sense of pride.

Reggie Rose stood up again. He had heard of UCLA *and* Southern Cal; maybe this coach was on to something. "If you could excuse me for just a moment," he said again.

He went to Mrs. Askew. Have you ever heard of a person named Vano Lucas?"

"Who?"

"Never mind." Reggie returned to the coach. As much as he enjoyed the notion of symmetry and revenue, this entire conversation about baseball pitchers and a refurbished stadium was giving him a headache. He was short with Radulski: "Thank you for coming. I'll take all of this under advisement."

With that, he dismissed the coach. Then took two Advil with a tall glass of water. While giving his temples a vigorous massage, he asked himself a pointed question: *could it be so easy?* A baseball pitcher enrolls at Entrada and brings with him millions of dollars in television revenue? *Could it be so easy?*

He made himself a note to speak with this coach again later, then turned his attention to the academic side of things. After all, according to Mrs. Askew, Entrada's curriculum deficiencies were at least as alarming as the revenue situation. Reggie decided he would put the academic dean to work. "After all," he said aloud, "To lead is to delegate."

But when he reached the office of the academic dean,

he found it empty. He charged on Mrs. Askew. "There's no one in the academic dean's office and all his things are cleared out," he declared.

"Naturally," answered the secretary. "In case you've forgotten, our academic dean left in May. He quit to go and live in Mexico with a 14-year-old *senorita* and write poetry about *Quetzalcoatl.*"

"I do remember. Now I do."

"Some of us think he went around the bend."

"I said I remember."

"All we have now is an interim dean. Oboe Meel."

"Oboe Meel?" Reggie flinched.

"Oboe is interim academic dean," Mrs. Askew reminded him. "Don't you remember?"

"I remember!" Reggie began to fume. "Will you stop asking me what I remember?" He made clenched fists before he said, "And where is Oboe Meel now, if I may be so bold?"

"He's probably out on the quad somewhere, basking in the sun. That's where he spends most of his time. That's where I'd look for him if I were you."

Oboe was indeed basking in the sun. Reggie found him on a park bench on the quad with two maintenance men, Billy Byrd and Sydney Gibbs. The most extraordinary event in Sydney's life had occurred two years earlier, when he had become the object of Mary Thorne's *heat.* In one week, they made love three times. For this, Sydney had achieved, in addition to the ecstasy of the experience itself, a considerable reputation. He had made it a point to broadcast his accomplishment wherever possible.

The most extraordinary event in Billy Byrd's life was winning a 56 dollar prize in the state lottery's *Instant Winner* game on March 2, 1978.

Oboe Meel's huge bulk occupied nearly three

quarters of the park bench. There was a small space near the end where Reggie could squeeze himself aboard. He informed Oboe that there was a lot of work to be done.

Oboe Meel opened his eyes a tiny bit. His thumbs were hooked under the straps of his coveralls. He spat out an arc of tobacco juice. "It would appear that being appointed academic dean, even on an interim basis, is going to be somewhat like having a pebble in the shoe. That is to say, an ongoing source of irritation."

"See here, Meel," said Reggie firmly. "There's a lot of work to be done. I could show you in the trustees' report."

Oboe opened his eyes a little wider before spitting out another tobacco arc. "We are *basking* here," he reminded Reggie. "If you must come into our presence, be so kind as to pick an appropriate topic of conversation for the circumstances. Besides which, I can assure you that trustees' reports are not real."

Reggie squinted against the morning sun and studied Oboe's enormous profile. Oboe was six feet, three inches tall, and weighed 375 pounds. He wore only Oshkosh B'Gosh coveralls, custom-made to fit his huge bulk. No shirt. He usually carried a large wad of Red Man chewing tobacco in his cheek. He wore black, high-top tennis shoes, unlaced, of EEE width, and no socks.

"Trustees' reports are not real," said Reggie Rose, repeating Oboe's observation. "And what is that supposed to mean, if I may ask?"

"It means precisely what it means. Trustees' reports are fictions. They are unreal."

Reggie took a sudden spur in the direction of quarrelsome: "I can assure you that the trustees' report is real. It has real pages and real data and a real hard cover. It also has a very discouraging prognosis."

Oboe Meel only giggled. In the fourth grade, his teacher had presented him with this conundrum: *If a tree falls in the forest, but there is no one to hear it fall, does it make any noise?* The need to deal with this question had so tormented Oboe that his education as such was largely completed at that point.

Throughout the rest of elementary school, junior high school, high school, college, and graduate school, Oboe fought with the riddle, answered it, framed it differently, thought about it, re-answered it, and dreamed about it. Eventually, he posed it this way: *what is real?*

This became Oboe's major breakthrough. Having thus framed the question, Oboe could divide everything in the whole wide world into one or the other category: the *real,* and the *not real.*

While it might have been true that Oboe spent most of his educational life never learning any new information, it was also true that he learned the successful techniques for camouflaging this fact. On any true-false, multiple choice, or essay question, Oboe could lead the professor through such a verbose labyrinth of the *real* and the *not real* that the professor was usually unable to slice through it at all. He learned countless ways to dialogue on his obsession so as to numb the history professor, the English professor, the science professor, and even the mathematics professor.

In this manner had Oboe Meel pounded out the terms of his own universe. His world was a fortress of conviction and a way of life. When Oboe assigned an item in the universe to one of his categories, that item was there to stay. He was thus intimidating in the minds of many people who knew him.

"See here, Meel, you accepted the appointment as interim academic dean. Why did you accept it if you don't plan to do any work, is what I'd like to know."

"I accepted it for extra money, not for extra work," answered Oboe, in round tones. "Would you care to have a look at this?" He handed Reggie a legal pad with questions scrawled in pencil on the top sheet.

"What is this supposed to be?"

"It is the preliminary stage of a philosophy test. Don't forget, I still have classes to teach."

Reggie asked him, "Are you teaching summer school?"

"Indeed not."

"Then why are you writing out philosophy tests? Why aren't you thinking up ways to enrich our curriculum?"

Oboe turned to face him: "*Post hoc facto. Post hoc ergo propter hoc. De Gustibus non disputandem est.*"

It sounded solid to Reggie Rose. "That's more like it," he observed. "Now I'll have a look at this test." But after skimming the questions written on the page he said, "These are multiple choice questions."

"That is correct," Oboe confirmed.

"How do you do it?"

"How do I do what?"

"How do you make multiple choice questions for a philosophy test?"

"Simple. I just make up the questions, then I determine the right answers."

Reggie read the first question: *Which is real, the blackbird singing, or just after?*

Mystified by this question, President Rose decided to move on to the next one: *If a coconut falls from a tree on a desert island, but only a sponge is near enough to hear it land, does the falling coconut in fact make any sound*?

"How can you answer questions like this?" asked Reggie.

Oboe Meel gave it a wave of the hand. "I don't have

the slightest idea. I merely add up all the answers, and the answer that gets the most votes wins. That becomes the right answer."

"Are you saying that the students end up choosing their own right answers?"

"A good way of putting it, I should think," commended Oboe.

Reggie could stand no more. Exhausted by the exigencies which this single morning had already wrought, he decided to think about what he would have for lunch. He said aloud, "If I eat lunch in the union, they might have that Waldorf salad they often make. It's usually quite nice."

Oboe approved of this approach: "Lunch is a very appropriate basking topic."

"Since this is Wednesday, they might have the veal *scallopini*."

Oboe reclosed his eyes just after rehooking his thumbs beneath the straps. He wheezed it out, "The veal dish is one of the union's better culinary efforts."

"But whenever I eat in the union," said Reggie, "Professor Revuelto always wants to join me. He seeks me out even if I don't make eye contact. He eats like a pig and sweats a lot."

"The wondrous dividend of basking is that there is always time to explore the alternatives."

"Of course, if my memory serves me, Revuelto is still in South America. And anything would be better than lunch with Bertie."

"Now you have it truly," rumbled Oboe in his richest, resonant tones. "You are right on target."

Chapter Two

Upon discovering that Vano had made a visit to Entrada College, Vernon Lucas was not pleased: "You did what??"

Vano repeated it: "I drove up to Entrada to visit. I went to their baseball field and talked to their coach."

Vernon, who was 73 years old but thought he was 72, said, "I can't believe what I'm hearing." He was turning red in the face. His pink scalp glistened through his thinning white hair. "Did I give you permission to visit Entrada College?"

"Nobody gave me permission. It was my own idea. Sort of."

"You don't have ideas!" snapped Vernon Lucas. "What you have is the world's livest arm. Ideas have no place in your life."

"Right." Vano slumped in his chair.

Vano's father poked his own sternum with a bony index finger. "I take care of the ideas. That's why I screen everything. Most hot-shot prospects have to go out and hire an agent, who usually screws everything up. We're sitting on a gold mine here, and it's your great good fortune to have me in charge of financial negotiations."

"Okay, okay."

"Why in hell would you want to go to college?"

"I don't want to go there," answered Vano.

"In the first place, Entrada College is nowhere. A

guy could sit on the bench at UCLA and get more attention from pro scouts than he could by being a superstar at a place like Entrada."

"Right," repeated Vano. "I don't want to go there anyway. What's in the second place?"

"Are you getting smart with me? Pay attention what I'm telling you. Do you want to pitch in a cow pasture with nobody watching? Do you want to spend four years doing homework? Do you realize that with your grades and test scores you would be ineligible to pitch because of Proposition 48? Do you have any knowledge at all of NCAA procedures for campus visits?"

Vano was confused by so many questions. He was pretty sure the answer to the first two was no, but he merely slumped a little deeper in his chair. "Right," he said.

Vernon Lucas asked, "Where did this Entrada idea come from, tell me that."

"I'm not sure where it came from. It was one of those days when I was getting vibes."

His father got even redder in the face and began to pace. "And that's another thing. If I hear about your *vibes* even one more time, I think I might have to vomit. Have you given any thought to my heart condition?"

Vano said, "Sister Cecilia was showing me a scrap book that had pictures of Mother with a holy man. It gave me some real heavy vibes. Before I knew it, I remembered that she went to Entrada."

"That does it," declared the senior Lucas. He snatched a nitroglycerine tablet and downed it rapidly. He summoned Sister Cecilia from the laundry room. "And make sure you bring that damned scrapbook with you," he commanded.

It was only a matter of moments before she arrived, clutching the scrapbook. She sat down in a chair next to

Vano. After Vano's father faced her off, he demanded to know the meaning of this.

"I was just cleaning out the attic," answered Sister quietly. "It's one of the things I'm paid to do. Cleaning, that is."

"Are you attempting sarcasm here?" But Vernon didn't wait for an answer. He grabbed the scrapbook and threw it open. "Do you have any idea who this freak is?" He was pointing to the holy man beside Vano's mother. Vano found himself moving in some low-level resonance, like the shallow end of the pool.

"No, I don't." said Sister Cecilia.

"His name was Alan Watts. I suppose you've never heard of him."

"No, I haven't." Sister was feeling humiliated.

Vano's father said, "Alan Watts was one of the biggest religious cuckoos who ever walked the planet. He preached the path of dropping out, burning incense, and contemplating your navel. Unfortunately, there were enough suckers like Vano's mother around to keep the bastard in business."

Sister Cecilia reminded Vernon that it was inappropriate to speak disrespectfully of the dead. She also asked him not to swear.

"I have no doubt he was a communist as well," added Vernon.

Sister assumed he hadn't heard her. "We shouldn't speak in a manner that dishonors the dead," she said.

"I heard you the first time. Vano's mother was a good kid, God rest her soul, but there wasn't an ounce of common sense in her. For charlatans like Alan Watts, she was easy prey. The facts are, she couldn't even balance a checkbook or understand the meaning of an escrow account. Why are the two of you slumped there like truants? Sit up straight."

Sister and Vano sat up straight.

Vernon told Sister, "I want all scrapbooks kept out of sight and out of mind. You hear me?"

Sister's eyes were lowered. "I didn't mean any harm. I only thought it might mean something to Vano if he could look at the pictures of his mother."

"There's no meaning in looking at pictures of a loony tune like Alan Watts."

"Where should I put the scrapbook?"

"Never mind, I'll take care of it myself. Now I want you both to listen up carefully. There's something important you need to know. Are you aware of anything? Do you ever watch the news?"

Vano wondered if the question was directed at him. "Who, me?"

"Yes, you. Of course, you."

Vano shrugged. "I'm not like into current events."

"Do you ever listen to the radio in that car I bought you?"

"Radios are for dweebs," Vano informed him. "I listen to tapes."

"Then you don't have a clue, do you?" With this snooty remark, Vernon shook his head slowly, then resumed his pacing.

Vano wondered where this conversation was headed when his father said, "It was on the news at noon. The Oakland A's traded three veteran players to the Yankees to get the first pick in the draft. Just to get the right to draft you."

Vano perked up his ears. "Three players? Who?"

"Harold Baines, Willie McGee, and Carney Lansford."

"Jesus Christ, those guys are superstars. They

traded all of them so they could get me?"

"Try to get this straight. It's really not over your head. They traded all three of them just to get the first pick in the draft. Plus a promising triple-a pitcher."

Vano was confused. "It's real confusing, isn't it?"

"And you were thinking about going to college. The point is we have the Oakland Athletics right where we want them. It's obvious that they are ready to deal in very big figures. Very, very big. Have you run your laps today?"

"No not yet."

"Then go run them."

*

July 18 was an open day in the schedule of the Oakland Athletics. It was a day of thick bay haze, heavy and humid, but by eleven a.m. when the haze burned off, it was hot.

The sun broke through on the A's sluggers, who were taking batting practice. Smashing line drives against the fence as well as over it. The crack of their bats echoed hollow in the empty Oakland Coliseum. Mark McGuire walloped two homers to deep left center. Then Jose Canseco, the 23-million dollar man, slammed one up against the left-center field fence. He followed that up with a tape-measure shot to dead center.

The Athletics were wearing their uniform pants and caps, but not their shirts; just undershirts. It was the same for Vano, who was warming up in the bullpen along the left field line. He wore his high school uniform pants and a gray tee shirt. On his head was the red team cap, with the white letters AV for Apple Valley.

Only 50 or 60 spectators, consisting of Oakland A's corporate brass, scouts, and minor league supervisory personnel, were permitted to watch this event. When the media people were turned away at the press gate, they concluded that something uniquely important was taking place on the inside.

And they were right. For Vernon Lucas, galvanized by his infinite belief in the transcendence of his only son's pitching arm, had goaded Oakland's team officials into an unheard-of proposition. Vano would pitch batting practice to the entire Athletics' lineup. *If even one hitter got one single hit,* Vano would agree to a ten million dollar signing bonus. If not, the signing bonus would be twenty million.

Vernon was sitting in one of the prime box seats behind home plate, next to Rakestraw, the Oakland general manager. It occurred to Rakestraw that one or two of the fine-print details still needed scripting. He asked Vernon, "How do we decide what's a hit?"

"You can decide," answered Vernon simply.

"I just want to be fair, that's all."

Vernon chuckled. "You'll be fair. You know a hit when you see one. Hell, if it makes you feel any better, you can put fielders out behind him. That would take the guess work out of it."

Then Rakestraw said, "Lucas, you've got balls this big, you know that? This big."

Lucas Senior's response was in the form of a stifled yawn. "So you keep saying."

The few observers who weren't in the home plate vicinity were stationed with their speed guns near the bullpen where Vano's warm-ups were popping the mitt of Jerome Neal, the Oakland A's bullpen coach and former major league catcher. Vano was throwing easily, just getting loose, topping out in the mid eighties. He had popped a sweat, though, and was beginning to feel grooved. He said so to Neal.

"What does that mean?"

"I'm loose and locked on. Pretty soon I'll start seeing every pitch before I throw it."

Neal wondered if Vano Lucas was a nut case. He shrugged and went back into his crouch. He had no idea what Vano was talking about, but he was close to finding out. Vano's next fast ball poured into his mitt at 99 per. Jerome Neal winced and flinched. While lobbing the ball back he said, "Jesus Christ, Kid, nice pop."

"There wasn't no pop on that," was Vano's scornful reply. "That wasn't even close to pop."

Neal reacted first by smiling, then by patronizing: "Yeah, sure, Kid. Right." He had read the stuff on Vano just like everybody else, but he assumed the stories were media hype or readings from faulty equipment.

But on the next fast ball, Neal saw his life pass before him. Picked up on all the guns at 112 or 114, it was a rocket that blazed into his mitt before he could react. A murmur rippled the gathered scouts while Neal stood up slowly. He whooshed his breath before he said, "Jesus Christ." Then he said to Vano, "Wait a minute, I'll be right back."

The Oakland veteran went directly to the dugout where he began by slipping a nut cup into position. Next, he put on the chest protector. He was strapping on the shinguards when Tony LaRussa, the A's field manager, approached. "Is he ready?" LaRussa asked.

"He didn't say he was."

"Then why are you putting on the gear?"

"Come and see," Neal replied.

LaRussa came to see. Neal brought his face mask down into position before he said, "Okay, Vano, go ahead."

Vano launched a dozen heaters which ranged from 108 to 118 miles per hour. They were like comets with angry tails, blurs that cracked the waiting mitt like cherry bombs. Then he threw a dozen of the 98 mile-an-hour sliders with the big bite, slamming into Neal's mitt ten inches off the ground. All in the strike zone.

Tony LaRussa wasn't speaking, but he was shaking his head. He thought to ask one of the scouts what the velocity was on his gun, but then he had another thought: *why bother*?

Neal explained to him, "I wish I could tell you I was *catchin'* this shit, Tony, but it's really just him hittin' the target."

LaRussa, who thought he had seen it all but now understood that he hadn't, couldn't find his tongue. He simply continued with the head shaking.

Vano's sweat was full broken. He told LaRussa, "I'm grooved and ready. Can we do it now?"

"Sure, Kid, let's do it right now."

Vano took his place on the mound. He looked slowly around the vast Oakland Coliseum but it didn't faze him; it could have been just another cow pasture next to another high school. Some of the A's took up defensive positions in no particular scheme, while others, the most famous ones, crowded around the batting cage. Standing next to Vano, Jerome Neal told him, "Don't be scared, Kid."

Vano couldn't think of anything to be afraid of. "What's to be scared of?" he asked Neal.

Since he had just been on the receiving end of Vano's best stuff, the veteran catcher wasn't surprised by this level of nonchalance. "It's just something you're supposed to say to young pitchers." Then Neal went ahead with some final instructions: "There won't be no signs. If you ever get the urge to throw something other than that heater, you just call me out here and tell me face to face. We straight on that?"

Vano said, "I don't want this thing here." He was pointing to the portable screen in front of the mound which was used for the protection of batting practice pitchers.

"The screen's just for protection."

"I don't care about protection, I care about bein' grooved. This thing will break my concentration."

Neal shrugged his shoulders before he motioned to two groundskeepers who removed the screen. Then the catcher took his place behind the plate, where Ricky Henderson, the all-star left fielder, had the lumber out. The umpire was a college official named Quinn, a friend of LaRussa's.

Ricky Henderson asked Neal, "Why'd you take the screen away?"

Neal was adjusting his face mask to double check its security. He said, "Lucas don't want it. I guess he figures ain't nobody gonna make contact."

This answer made Henderson furious. He locked his spikes in deep and tightened his grip on the bat handle. "I'm gonna wire this pale motherfucker up," he announced.

From his crouch Neal said, "Get ready for some high heat."

This second insult was more astonishing than the first to Henderson. "You tellin' me what's comin'?! Are you crazy??"

Neal just laughed while Henderson turned his notorious glare on Vano Lucas. Vano didn't see the glare, though. What he saw was the pitch complete, before he even threw it. He saw its beginning, its middle, and its end. He saw its velocity as well as its track.

Vano went slowly into his wind-up. The pitch exploded up and in to Henderson so fast it seemed like warp speed. The Oakland all-star was paralyzed. Quinn, the umpire, exclaimed "HoooHaaa!" which everyone understood to mean *strike one*.

The shaken Henderson stepped out of the box to try and regroup. He took a few seconds with the pine tar and longed for focus. It proved to be an exercise in futility, however, for when he stepped back inside the batter's box it was the same result. The second pitch froze him like the first. On the third delivery, he managed a feeble, late swing, then went straight to the dugout without a word.

The next batter, Terry Steinbach, went down on three straight pitches without removing the bat from his shoulder.

In his comfortable seat, Vernon Lucas was cackling. He asked Rakestraw if he'd seen enough.

"That's only two batters."

"I can count," was Vernon's reply. "Let me know when you've seen enough."

Rakestraw didn't answer, but made a be-quiet gesture with the palm of his hand. The Oakland hitters went down one by one, like sheep in the chute. Most of them were called out, while others managed a late swing or two, of the impotent variety. Dave Henderson took a swing at every pitch, but made no contact.

On his second at-bat, Mark McGuire hit one foul tip. Then he was called out on a 115-mile an hour blazer low and away. Vano had pitched through the entire line-up twice without allowing even one fair ball to be hit. He signaled to Neal, who came to the mound. "I need a break," Vano complained. "This is like pitchin' six innings straight."

Neal informed Rakestraw who said, "Let's not only give him a break, let's give him a check. We know what we're lookin' at here, the kid is unhittable."

That would have been the end of it, except LaRussa

informed that Jose Canseco was insisting on one more chance. He was demanding a third at-bat.

Rakestraw turned to Vernon Lucas to ask him what he thought.

"If he's not too tired to throw to another hitter, it's okay." said Vernon. "You'll have to ask him. Go ahead and get your checkbook out, though."

"Ask him," Rakestraw said tersely to Jerome Neal.

When Neal asked Vano if he felt up to throwing to one more hitter, Vano was annoyed. But he said okay. "Who is it?" he wanted to know.

"Canseco wants one more chance."

Vano popped his gum. "Okay. One fast ball, one slider, and then a change."

"You throw a change?"

"I've got a circle change. I like to throw it once in a while, just for fun. Let's not just strike him out, let's make him look bad."

Jerome Neal was grinning. "You seen a batter yet didn't look bad?"

"Hey, give me a break here; I just wanna throw it."

Neal was still grinning. A lifetime .181 hitter during his checkered big-league career, he was getting no small satisfaction watching the overpaid, overindulged superstars overmatched. "Sounds good, Kid. Just make sure you remember the order."

The first pitch was a laser, up and in. Canseco took a very late, albeit ferocious swing. He missed. He pounded his bat on the plate in frustration. The slider he hadn't seen; it froze him for strike two.

There were no vibes, yet Vano still took a lingering look at the clouds before he threw the change, which he was careful to keep down and away. At a mere 85 miles per hour, it approached Canseco like slow motion. So far out in front was the Oakland slugger that he nearly disclocated his spine. He took a hopeless swing while striving in vain to keep his hands back.

The bat flew out of his hands.

Vano didn't see it coming, at least not right away. It helicoptered its way in a twirling arc in his direction. When he did see it, it was too late to react. The big end of the *Louisville Slugger* nailed him right between the eyes, precipitating a festival of lights in his brain. Vano went down hard like a dropsack on a loose tether.

The impact of the pitching rubber did some modest damage to the lumbar region of his back, but he was unaware of it. He was out cold.

*

Vano's coma lasted 30 days. After three weeks, during which time he showed no sign of improvement, the doctor explained to Vernon that they might have to move him to a rehabilitational facility in Modesto.

"Why?"

"It's a facility which specializes in long-term care. This hospital is no longer appropriate."

"You think you're going to warehouse him, in other words. Do I have any say in this?"

"No." Then the doctor said, "It might be time to start thinking about some difficult decisions."

"What's that supposed to mean?"

"If he continues to show no sign of recovery, you may want to ask yourself how long we should continue with this intravenous feeding."

Vernon Lucas was appalled. "Are you out of your

fucking mind?? Do you have any idea who this is?"

"He's your son, I believe."

"This is Vano Lucas! He's got the greatest arm in the game! Maybe in the *history* of the game!"

"It's never an easy situation to confront," murmured the doctor.

For her part, Sister Cecilia burst into tears and left the room. She made her way to the hospital chapel where she lit candles and worried her way feverishly through the rosary.

In his coma, Vano was a *tabula rasa*. He might have been dead. Until the 28th day, that is, when he fluttered some modest brain activity which triggered occasional moments of subconscious and semi-conscious perception. A mental picture of a terraced pyramid with urban flavor somehow, but so indistinct in its definition as if it sat behind a scrim. It was an image which repeated itself from time to time in his elliptical brain like a dream, only lacking even the *de facto* sequencing of a dream.

On his way back to consciousness, Vano surfaced by way of an intense telepathic journey through time and space. He was zooming through the universe. It may have lasted only a few moments, but since time was suspended, it seemed like a lengthy event. He was passing at incredible speed through a zone of laser beams and particles of light.

At first there seemed to be no pattern to the twinkling. There was nothing beneath his feet that he could see, yet he felt himself supported somehow. He found himself in a chamber of sorts where light patterns suggested walls, then quickly vanished. Coalitions of light points defined the presence of evanescent human-like shapes.

Vano heard a voice: "Welcome." The voice seemed to have as its source one of the shapes, but the shapes twinkled in and out, and not always in the same spot.

The voice spoke again: "You will know us as particle people. That is not a name we use, but earth humanoids, dwelling in the ego mode, are usually comforted by a system of labeling." The diction was so clean and firm. Vano thought the voice sounded like the radio announcer on the midnight to six A.M. shift. Each of the particle people had an occasional head region, but nothing resembling a mouth. He couldn't tell which of the particle people was speaking at any given moment.

The particle voice continued by saying, "Our way of life is the way of complete harmony with the ebb and flow of the universe. We are able to reduce ourselves to the billions of atomic particles of which we, like all matter, are constituted. In this diffuse state, we float through the universe as particle dust, each atomic particle a microcosm of the total organism. We live in concord with the entire span of the electromagnetic spectrum. When there may be cause, we are able to reconvene our atomic particles, so to speak, in a sort of committee of the whole. It is then that we assume these humanoid forms. Now you understand the fundamental principle of particle mode existence."

Vano Lucas wasn't sure he understood anything. He could see countless stars in all directions. He could see nothing when he looked down, yet he still felt something firm underfoot. The walls, though transparent, were visible from time to time, just like the particle humanoids themselves. He wondered how he got here, and what he was doing here.

"You are here because the vibrations you have known from time to time have led you to the threshold of *hooommm*, if only on a superficial plane. You have the capacity, or so we believe, to go beyond."

Hooommm? Vano wondered. Since they were able to know his thoughts, it occurred to him that the particle people might be God.

The particle voice seemed to reside in his brain as well as without: "We are not God. We can know your thoughts because we are blended with the whole electromagnetic spectrum. Dwellers on Earth are fond of imagining a huge creature like themselves, who lives in the sky. They call this imaginary creature God. It is a predictable and, in some respects, necessary compensation because the way of life for humanoids on Earth is the ego mode. It includes only a very tiny fraction of the spectrum. There is no self but the ego, and very little freedom from the demands made by this self. The energy needed to maintain the ego mode is its own support system. Now you understand the fundamental principle of ego mode existence."

But Vano's head was swimming. It was plain to him that he was hearing only parts of what the particle people were telling him, and his understanding of what he did hear was so limited.

"Do not worry," the particle voice instructed him. "Everything we are telling you will lodge in your memory bank. Which parts become available to your conscious mind will, of course, depend on your development. The point of emphasis is that *hooommm* is a zone in response to the ego mode, but it is also part of a larger process which, at this point, remains beyond your ken. This is a partial understanding of the actual meaning of existence. Someday, your understanding may be complete."

And then in an instant, the particle people were gone. Vano felt himself whisked away at unimaginable speed, surrounded once again by the darkness and the flashing laser beams.

Awake and alert in the aftermath of this cosmic downhill, he rolled onto his side in the hospital bed. There were strong vibrations to rattle the cage of this tenuous consciousness. His hospital room seemed pellucid with an orange haze. Even so, he could make out clearly the two women seated near the window, wearing salmon hospital smocks.

He was looking at them, but immersed in crossword puzzles, they failed to notice his brand-new body language. Vano's *hooommm* was still a dull roar, and the two women seemed so far away. "I think I've been someplace," he announced in a loud voice.

The startled women turned to look. "Did you say something? Are you awake?"

Vano repeated it, after a pause: "I think I've been someplace."

*

Driving his brand new Lincoln Town Car, Vernon Lucas took Vano home from the hospital. Other than the lack of stamina associated with his weakened condition, Vano seemed to be feeling just fine. The new automobile had burgundy velour seats and a busy instrument panel which looked extremely high tech. His father asked him how he liked the car.

After a pause Vano said, "It's real nice, Dad."

Vernon had never heard his son call him *Dad* before. He went ahead nevertheless, "I got it up at Thornton's in Victorville. Railsback took 2500 dollars off the sticker price, or I wouldn't have been interested. I really don't need a new car, since the Buick was only a year old, but when someone makes you an offer like that, it's hard to pass up."

Vano was in a comfort zone of low but firm

resonance. It was *hooommm*. When he finally spoke, it was only to repeat himself: "It's real nice, Dad."

"You see this?" asked Lucas Senior. He pointed to a small blue button on the steering column.

"I see it," said Vano.

"Why are your answers taking so long? Are you paying attention? This button activates a read-out panel; it's computer operated. Give you about any data you can think of." Saying this, he pushed the button, which produced an illuminated green rectangular screen above the radio console. Yellow digital letters and numbers indicated the vehicle's speed, current fuel efficiency in miles per gallon, the time, the date, revolutions per minute of the engine, exact running temperature, and several other pieces of information Vano couldn't be sure about.

Looking at this glut of data, Vano felt an uncomfortable flicker, but then it went away.

"Railsback told me the computer panel was the cat's meow, and anybody who has one doesn't want to do without it. It was slick, the way he was trying to gouge me for the few extra bucks, but I told him if I was going to pay for it, the deal was off. He was more or less over a barrel then, because he knew I didn't really need the car anyway; the bottom line is, he threw it in for no extra cost."

Then Vernon stopped talking about the car. Vano wondered what to think about the computer read-out panel. Eventually he said, "It's real nice, Dad."

Lucas Senior decided that ought to be enough small talk. It was time to broach the most salient topic: "How soon do you think you'll be ready to pitch again?"

Another lengthy pause transpired before Vano said, "I remember pitching baseball."

"You remember pitching baseball? Did I hear you right?"

"Yes. I do. I believe my memory is intact."

"What did that blow to the head *do* to you?" Vernon Lucas felt his blood pressure escalating to a higher level. "*You remember pitching baseball*?? That's like saying Michael Jordan remembers making a basket!"

Approximately five seconds passed before Vano said, "I can't remember who Michael Jordan is."

Vernon's agitation intensified beyond his best intentions. "I don't know what zone you've been in for the last month, but I've been in the combat zone. I've been fending off questions from the Oakland management, legal inquiries from soft drink companies, nagging from the media, and prayer requests from Sister Cecilia. We're going to have to talk a little turkey here. With all due respect for your condition, of course."

"How is Sister Cecilia doing?" Vano heard himself asking. But then he felt himself retreating down the corridor of *hooommm* to a place of deeper reverberations. He said again, "I can remember pitching."

"Do you remember pitching to the Oakland A's? Do you remember blowing them away in the Coliseum?"

Eventually, when the answer arrived, it was "Yes." But Vano discovered that even when his memories were clear, there were no emotional attachments associated with them. They were utterly neutral, like recollecting the turns you might take along a route to reach a particular destination.

Vernon continued aggressively, "Then maybe you remember what's at stake? The gold mine is still out there waiting. When do you suppose you'll be ready to do some throwing?"

Vano pondered the question, but without urgency, in a condition of total serenity. "When it sounds like it might be fun?" he asked, by way of answering.

"Fun?!" sputtered Vernon. "Did you say *fun*??" His

crescendoing level of frustration warned him to slow down. As luck would have it, they were on the outskirts of Bakersfield, where he had a favorite restaurant. He swung the car into the parking lot of *The Cut Above*.

The Cut Above had subdued lighting and a decor to suggest the turn of the century. Vano's father stopped at the bar long enough to order two dry martinis. He downed one in a hurry, then carried the other to their table. On the table was a kerosene lamp, but it wasn't burning; it was only for looks.

The waitress came. Vano's father ordered garden salad and braised sirloin tips on toast, cooked in wine sauce. He told the waitress, "And one more of these martinis. Dry. Make that right away, please."

When it was his turn, Vano said, "I'd like a cheeseburger, please."

"Oh come on," complained his father. "Is that what you're going to order?"

Vano felt another of the uncomfortable flickers before the answer came to him. "They didn't have cheeseburgers in the hospital, I think I'd enjoy one."

"How do you know what they fed you in the hospital? You were eating through a tube."

Briefly, "I'm pretty sure it wasn't cheeseburgers."

"That's not something you order in a place like this. You can get a cheeseburger at Burger King, for god's sake. This menu has a large selection. Maybe you'd better look it over again."

The waitress stood with her pad and pencil poised while Vano tried to peruse the menu again. He wanted to think of a reply, but these things seemed to come or they didn't. He found himself flickering again, just before going numb. Finally his father instructed the waitress, "I guess you might as well bring him a cheeseburger."

There was no conversation during the meal. Vano thought the cheeseburger tasted very good. When they were finished eating, Vernon ordered coffee.

The waitress brought the coffee.

"Oh come on," complained Vernon Lucas to the waitress. "When I order coffee, I want a *real* cup. This cup is only half full."

Vano took a disinterested look at the cup, in which the brown liquid rose to a level one half inch below the brim. The waitress said quietly, "With all due respect, Sir, I'd say it's more than half full."

"I don't want half a cup, I want a full cup when I order coffee."

"I'd be happy to bring you some more, Sir."

"Well of course."

She went to get the pot. During her absence, Vernon said to his son, "Let's see if we can negotiate some kind of a timetable."

Vano wasn't sure what a timetable would mean, but he could tell that his father was ready to return to the subject of pitching baseball. "Timetable?"

"That's what I said. Timetable. When you might be able to start throwing, a little at a time to start with, then working on up. Are you with me on this?"

The waitress returned to their table with the pot and painstakingly brought Vernon's cup right up to the brim. "That's more like it," Vano's father said to her. "That's what I call a full cup. Thank you."

Vano was observing this exchange from deep in. His father and the waitress were now miniature figures on the far side of a vast and bland landscape. With no stress whatsoever, Vano wondered what his answer to the timetable question would turn out to be.

As it happened, it was moot. Using both hands,

Vano's father lifted the brimming cup toward his lips with trembling fingers. When he burned his mouth, his hands began to shake. The scalding coffee washed down over both his hands. The cup fell clattering to the saucer while the old man screeched in pain. Beads of sweat formed quickly on his scarlet scalp. Vano watched his father flap his hands to shed some of the pain while the coffee soaked deep into the tablecloth.

*

Vano spent the bigger part of August in a state of unattached tranquility, physically as well as psychically. The comfort zone of *hooommm* seemed to fit him like a glove. He enjoyed the lassitude of the condo deck, with its warm southern exposure and firm mountain view. He read a good many books, reflectively, books such as *Kon-Tiki*, by Thor Heyerdahl, *The Snow Leopard* by Peter Matthiesen, and *In My Own Way* by Alan Watts.

"What will you do if you're not a baseball pitcher?" Sister Cecilia asked him one day.

Vano looked up slowly from his reading, taking the necessary time to absorb the question. "I'm not sure," he said.

"Will you get a job?"
"I don't know."
"Maybe you could."
"That would be nice."
"You're so agreeable, Vano; do you know that?"

Eventually Vano replied, "I never thought about it. Yes, I guess I am agreeable."

Sister found no discomfort in the long pauses which

delayed his answers. She enjoyed the newer, gentler Vano. In fact, although she would never say so to his father, she felt relief in his apparent liberation from the reckless, aggressive male mode. She asked him about college.

"It might be nice to go to college," he replied.

"Maybe you could go to Entrada. You visited there."

"That would be nice."

"Letters keep coming from that baseball coach you talked to. But your grades in high school were low, Vano, and it seems late to be applying."

What Sister was saying was true. There was no reply which occurred to him. His *hooommm* was ultra firm.

She continued, "Maybe you could still get in. Maybe it's not too late to apply to junior college."

After another substantial delay Vano told her, "I think I would enjoy going to college."

None of this serenity registered on Vano's father, however. Vernon was engaged in a desperate cycle of damage-control activities day and night. When he wasn't on the phone with doctors and lawyers, he was stalling Oakland Athletics' personnel or product endorsement opportunities. He acted as Vano's press secretary, to field the ongoing but dwindling calls from press people and other media.

The Oakland general manager visited Vano once on the deck to remind him about the signing bonus.

"We already have a lot of money in this house," Vano told him.

"It wouldn't take much," countered Rakestraw. "I know you're not in shape, but if you could demonstrate that you can still throw, there's still a lot of money on the table."

Vano pointed out that he didn't feel any desire to be a pitcher. Then he asked the GM if he'd ever had the pleasure of reading *Kon-Tiki*.

This irrelevant question prompted Rakestraw to try a

more manipulative approach: "I traded three guys to get you. Three proven major leaguers, I might add."

These remarks, meant to provoke in Vano a sense of guilt, fell short of their goal. Vano felt a serene indifference to anything Rakestraw might have to say. He finally answered, "Maybe the three players will be happy with their new team."

The frustrated Rakestraw knew when it was time to fold. On the way out he said to Vernon Lucas, "I see what you mean."

"You don't have a clue," was the dispirited father's reply.

Vernon paid Gomez and Ann-Marie five hundred dollars apiece to see what they could do, but Gomez could offer only baseball, and Ann-Marie, sex. Vano obliged Ann-Marie, and he played catch with Gomez, both without engagement. He was firm in his understanding that sex and baseball were activities of the ego connection, and not capable of providing any lasting satisfaction.

At the end of the month Vernon Lucas threw up his hands in disgust and permitted Vano to enroll at Entrada College. "At least it'll get him away from home," he muttered to Sister. Entrada was an institution in need of students, as it happened, so Vano's substandard high school record was no obstacle. As long as he could pay the cost, the school would be happy to admit Vano, and of course, his father had plenty of money.

*

The night before he was to leave for college, Vano was alone in the den watching the TV news when Sister

Cecilia came home from Salvation Army band practice. She fussed around in the kitchen for half an hour or so. By the time the late news was over, she came into the den and sat next to Vano on the couch. "I can't get used to the idea that you're going away to college. You're going to be gone for a long time, Vano; I'm going to miss you."

"I'll miss you too, Sister Cecilia."

"It's going to be pretty lonely around here."

After a delay of a few seconds Vano said, "Sister, I thought you were Catholic."

"Of course I'm *Catolico*; the Salvation Army band is just an outside activity I enjoy." She couldn't help but like him this way, though. "It's a very thoughtful observation for you to make, Vano."

He waited again before speaking, "Maybe you could come to Entrada for a visit sometime. It might help to alleviate the loneliness."

"It's getting late, Vano, and I'm awfully tired. How would you like to tuck me into bed?"

Sister had never asked him a question like this before. "I never thought about it," he said.

In her eyes were unfamiliar pinpoints of light as she told him, "I think it would be awfully nice if you would."

Vano felt a flickering like a train passing rapidly through a station, but the moment passed. When he found his tongue he said, "Okay then, I guess."

They went up to Sister Cecilia's bedroom. After she seated Vano on the edge of the bed, she got a pink nylon nightgown from her dresser and laid it beside him. Then, facing him, she said, "I'm ready now."

Vano felt more of the flickering in spite of, or perhaps because of, the fact he was getting aroused. After a few moments he asked, "How do we go about this?"

"Well, I can't very well put my nightgown on if I'm

still wearing my clothes, can I?"

Vano started some heavy breathing. It was hard to determine where the anomaly was more peculiar in this intimate encounter--Sister's determination or his reluctance. Eventually, he found his fingers on the top brass button of Sister's navy blue wool Salvation Army jacket. Slowly, he unbuttoned them one after the other until he was able to help her slip the jacket off.

She closed her eyes as he removed her white blouse and her white bra; her large breasts tumbled free. Sister Cecilia was slightly overweight, but voluptuous. She tilted her head back and began combing her fingers through her long, black hair.

Vano removed her Salvation Army skirt and then, after some substantial hesitation, he slid her nylon underpants all the way down to her ankles. Sister stepped out, took hold of the back of his head, then pulled his face in against her stomach.

Vano smelled Sister's flesh mingled with the sweet fragrance of baby powder. He put his arms around her and let his hands travel the slick contours of her generous hips. Aroused though he was, he found there was still a tenuous location in a flickering *hooommm*. He asked Sister Cecilia if he was supposed to put her nightgown on now.

But she answered, "I can't help myself, Vano; I have to have you."

They made love on her bed. The lovemaking gave him so much pleasure it separated him from the comfort zone. He wondered if he might be better off to stay at home instead of going off to college.

About five minutes after her convulsive orgasm, Sister sat up so she could begin squirming into her nightgown. "We must never do this again, Vano," she declared. "It's evil."

Vano could feel himself receding deeper, deeper down. He didn't reply.

"It's terribly, terribly evil," said Sister again.

"I see."

"This whole month I've wanted you, but the Lord has made His will known to me. And now I've gone right ahead and disobeyed."

Hooommm it was, deep and firm.

"That's what true wickedness is," Sister continued, "Willful disobedience. We must never do this again."

Still, Vano didn't speak. She was so distant, so way down the wrong end of the binoculars.

The next thing she said was, "Please go to your room now, Vano."

Vano went to his room, trailing his blue jeans and underwear behind. When he went to sleep, he had the dream again. It was the pyramids, but not the pyramids exactly, because there were terraces. Whatever it was it was large, and streaked with gold from the dawn's early light.

When he woke up, he pondered the dream. Maybe it was a sign of some kind, or maybe it came from the particle people. But no, didn't he have the dream the first time before there was ever an encounter with them?

If the dream was about the pyramids, then the water could be the Nile, but how could the place be Egypt if there wasn't any sand? Whenever he had the dream, it seemed to provoke the same questions. What was it the particle people said to him? *Some day your understanding may be complete.* Vano felt not a sliver of frustration owing to the uncertainty; he was lodged in the deepest, firmest *hooommm* he'd ever known.

Sister Cecilia helped him pack his suitcases. She was uncomfortable, Vano could see it in her eyes. But for him there was no discomfort at all. The process of packing beside her was all neutral, about like counting boxcars on a passing freight train.

Chapter Three

A campus host showed Vano to his dorm when he moved in. One of his roommates, a bookish young man named Arnold Beeker, was already there. Arnold wore thick glasses with black frames reinforced by chunks of adhesive tape. His tapes and CDs were classical music. He was in the process of setting up his computer next to the reference books arranged neatly on his study desk. "You have a funny name," he said to Vano.

"Sure." Vano smiled.

"What does it mean?"

"What does what mean?"

"Your name," answered Arnold Beeker. "What does it mean?"

It never occurred to Vano that a person's name was supposed to mean something. Besides, he was deep in. After a few moments he said, "I don't know. I never thought about it."

"Since we're going to be roommates," said Arnold, "You'd probably like to know all about me."

"That would be nice."

"First of all," Arnold began, "I'm one of those peoople that bad things happen to. My father says I'm a regular *Joe Blitzflick*. I don't know who that is, but it's probably a character from a comic strip. My father spends a lot of time reading the comics."

Vano didn't say anything.

Arnold went on, "Sometimes he even uses the highlighter on the comics. He always says he doesn't want to be standing too close to me when the shooting starts, if you know what I mean."

Vano didn't know what he meant, but decided not to reply. Arnold continued by disclosing some of his remarkable theories about the universe and its mysteries. He had run most of these through one program or another on his computer, and he kept the results on floppy disk, for purposes of privacy.

For instance, Arnold Beeker believed that creatures from outer space observed most of North America from invisible space ships. These creatures were involved in cosmic research. He further believed that *outer space* was really a country in Eastern Europe with a different atmosphere. He further believed that the creatures who lived there had soft plastic instead of skin, and electric wires instead of bones.

Arnold was free to admit that his espousal of these and other similar theories had exposed him to harsh ridicule over time.

But Vano Lucas found no basis for objecting to any of the theories. When Arnold told him about the creatures in Eastern Europe with electric wires instead of bones, Vano said, "That sounds great, Arnold."

"You mean you really think it's possible?"

"Sure, Arnold. It sounds real possible to me."

Overjoyed at this acceptance and approval, Arnold said, "I can tell we're going to be fast friends. All my life people have called me a nerd because of my beliefs and the way I look. Have you ever been called a nerd?"

This was a hard one; Vano had to think. Finally he said, "I can't remember that I ever was. No."

"You don't look like a nerd, but you sort of act like

one. Have you ever been called a geek?"

"I don't think so. I can't remember for sure."

It didn't seem to matter much to Arnold, who was wearing a wide grin. "We'll be nerds of a feather," he said earnestly. "I can tell we're going to be fast friends."

Vano wondered if, in the interest of honesty, he should reveal to Arnold how recently he had been one of the arrogant bastards who treat nerds with contempt and relish making their lives miserable. It also occurred to him that Arnold might take some delight in hearing about the particle people encounter. He was in a relatively deep zone, though, and there would be the problem of sequencing the information.

The arrival of the third roommate, Robin Snook, changed the agenda altogether. He was a football player. He was six feet, two inches, approximately the same height as Vano, but a great deal bulkier, at 230 pounds of muscle mass. Robin had a round, open face, and short-cropped hair.

As soon as the introductions went around, Robin said, "You're Vano Lucas? Are you serious?"

When Vano amitted that he was, Robin turned to Arnold Beeker and declared, "I *know* this guy!"

"You know him already?"

"I mean I know who he is. He brings the high heat. Everybody knows who he is."

Arnold wondered why *he* didn't know. He also wondered what was meant by *high heat.* It might be some kind of a thermal device, but he couldn't say. Eventually, Vano told him quietly, "I used to be a baseball pitcher, Arnold. I think Robin is referring to that."

"He used to be a baseball pitcher," laughed Robin Snook. "That's like saying Joe Montana used to be a quarterback. What do you mean, *used to?* Aren't you on the team?"

The delay which preceded Vano's answer was long and tedious. "I can't imagine any pleasure in it."

"Shit, this guy almost signed with the A's. Everybody wanted to sign him."

"I had no idea," Arnold murmured.

The conversation might have worked its way into Vano's accident and recovery, but it turned out that Robin Snook was a sports celebrity in his own right. As a football star out of high school, he'd been recruited by UCLA, Southern Cal, San Diego State, Washington, and Colorado, to name but a few.

"But you chose Entrada?" asked Arnold.

"I wanted to play right away. I don't want to waste my time redshirting or being somebody's back-up. Know what I mean?"

Arnold had no idea what *redshirting* might imply, but what he did know was that he was now rooming with two famous jocks. Some of the attention and adulation which was certain to flow in their direction might flow on over and anoint him, too. Of the two, Robin was clearly the better interview. "What's your position?" Arnold asked him.

"Tailback," answered Robin Snook.

"But you look big enough to play the line."

"Who wants to be a grunt? There's no glory in the line. I want to carry the ball and score touchdowns."

"I can see your point," Arnold admitted.

On the second day of rush week, Robin, Vano, and Arnold were headed for the afternoon mixer at the Chi house. Vano could generate no enthusiasm for fraternity life, but Arnold was smitten with the prestige which the Greek system seemed to offer.

"I'd feel a lot better if you went with me," he told Vano. "I've never had much luck in social situations."

Vano tried to imagine social skills inferior to those which he currently possessed. Nevertheless, he told Arnold, "I'd be happy to go with you."

"I'm sure it would give me more confidence."

"I'd be happy to go with you, Arnold."

En route, the three stopped at the curb to wait for a passing steamroller at an intersection which was being resurfaced. "I really and truly think I might get a bid," said Arnold Beeker, thinking no such thing.

Vano wondered if any fraternity would really want Arnold as part of its membership, but Robin Snook exclaimed, "That's the stuff! Always think positive!" For emphasis, he gave Arnold a whack on the back. The impact knocked Arnold's glasses onto the pavement, where the steamroller smashed them to smithereens. Picking up the powdery remains in disbelief, Arnold cupped them in his hands. "Now what am I going to do?"

"Have no fear," counseled Robin. "Just follow me."

But as soon as they reached the lawn of the Chi house, Robin was swallowed up by a crowd of active backslappers, who started feeding him barbecued chicken and large drafts of *Bud Lite*. He began devouring a hefty leg and thigh quarter.

Vano and Arnold were left to stand by themselves. "They're going to put me on the yoyo patrol," Arnold lamented. "I just know they are."

Comfortably in *hooommm*, Vano needed six seconds to process his reply: "What is the yoyo patrol?"

"That's where they take you off by yourselves with all the other geeks and dweebs who won't get a bid. They put you all together so they can keep you out of the way."

"I see."

"Where's Robin, anyway?"

Vano explained, "He's eating barbecued chicken and getting slapped on the back by a large group of juniors and seniors."

Then a suave looking junior by the name of Skip Leslie approached them. He wore a blue blazer with the Chi crest. Had he realized who Vano Lucas was, he might have chosen a different strategy, but he judged him by the appearance of his companion. "I'd like you fellows to follow me this way, if you don't mind."

They followed Skip Leslie to the basement of the Chi house, where the recreation room was located. Since he was nearly blind without his glasses, Arnold kept a firm grip on Vano's shirttail all the way.

The recreation room was quiet and dimly lit. Someone was showing a video tape of Chi history. Vano and Arnold took seats beside Rusty and Toby. Rusty had a marine haircut; he wore green camouflage fatigues, a maroon beret, and glossy combat boots. Toby had shoulder-length blond hair and a full beard. He wore rubber tire sandals and a hopsack tunic with peacocks embroidered on the front.

Arnold asked Vano to describe them. Vano described Rusty first, then Toby.

"I knew it," Arnold declared. "This is the yoyo patrol." He turned in the general direction of Skip Leslie to ask, "This is the yoyo patrol, isn't it?"

"You bet it is," was Leslie's answer.

Then Arnold asked if he could have some of the barbecued chicken.

"We'll have to see if there's any left, a little later on," said Skip. And then he left.

In deep and firm, Vano watched the videotape. It was educational, but not engaging.

Later in the afternoon, on the way back to the dorm,

Vano and Arnold stopped at the student union for a soft drink. Arnold stumbled by mistake into the women's restroom. He spent several moments hunting for a urinal, then gave up the search in disgust. He decided to use one of the stalls.

The stall he chose was occupied by Rita Lieberman, who was a very aggressive female. Rita made not a sound but delivered a blow across the bridge of Arnold's nose with the spine of her hardbound dictionary. The impact left Arnold semi-conscious.

*

The first football game of the season was against Las Lagrimas College. It was late in the second quarter when Robin entered the game at tailback. Entrada was already trailing by a score of 20-0. In the huddle, quarterback Howard Leslie, who called himself Skip, said, "Robin, I'm calling your number right now. We'll run the 28 off tackle." His name was not actually Skip, and nobody called him that, but he had adopted it as a nickname because he thought it appropriate for a quarterback.

Robin carried the ball off tackle and gained 12 yards. He bashed over two linebackers in the process. A modest cheer rippled the small crowd.

In the huddle, Leslie said, "Let's run that again."

They tried it again, only this time Robin gained 25 yards. He knocked flat a linebacker and a cornerback, then barged over the top of a safety. This time the fans were more vocal in their appreciation.

"Jesus Christ," said Leslie. "Can you do that every time?"

"Of course," grinned Robin. "But it's too easy. I'd like to try it once with no blocking. Just give me the ball, and everybody drop to the ground. That's the way I'd like to try it."

The other players in the huddle snorted their astonishment. "What the hell are you talkin' about?" demanded Leslie.

"Look," Robin pleaded. "It's too easy with all this blockin'. I'd like to give it a try with no blockin'."

"You are out of your fucking mind, aren't you?"

Robin explained. "I have this mental picture. I see myself smashing and weaving my way through their whole team, without any blocks. Come on, Howard, let me try it just this once."

"It's not Howard, it's Skip."

"Okay, Skip, what d'you say?"

"What the hell," growled Kowalski, the right guard, who hated to block, "Let him try it. It's no skin off our ass." The connection between the game itself and Kowalski's mind was indeed a tenuous one. He knew that Mary Thorne was up in the stands somewhere, and he wished like everything he was up there with her. Then he wished like everything he was in bed with her. The longer he allowed this fantasy to linger in his mind's eye, the more glazed his eyes became. Until finally, Howard (Skip) Leslie had to take him by the elbow and guide him to the line of scrimmage.

They tried it just this once, Robin Snook carrying the ball on the 28 off tackle with no blocking. He got smeared. He was tackled simultaneously by eight players, who smothered him and gouged him and even punched him until they nearly buried him in the turf.

Up in the stands, a leather-lunged woman named Grizelda bellowed: "Vass is loss?? Haff you effer hurt of any blokink?!" Just to make sure the players heard her, she yelled it a second time.

In Section BB, Vano was describing each play to Arnold Beeker. Arnold's new glasses were in his pocket, but he couldn't wear them because his eyes and nose were still swollen from his encounter with Rita Lieberman's dictionary. "Robin didn't gain any yardage that time," Vano told Arnold.

"That's too bad," Arnold replied. "Why not?"

After five seconds Vano said, "I'm not sure, but it looked like there wasn't much blocking."

"How do they expect him to gain yardage without any blocking?"

Vano was in too deep, and anyway, it was the kind of question which didn't need an answer.

Elsewhere in the stands sat Wilfong Weingrad, 87 years old. Wilfong, one of Entrada's wealthiest and most eccentric alumni, wore a burgundy silk smoking jacket, the tail of which extended from beneath the hem of his threadbare college letter jacket. His glazed, knobby fingers were nearly translucent, while his face was like a wrinkled, pale prune. Wilfong Weingrad cared not a whit for football. He lived on the edge of hysteria.

His housekeeper, Grizelda, sat next to him, wearing a long overcoat, even though the temperature was 86 degrees Farenheit. She wore the overcoat because it had large pockets, the better to house her pints of Jim Beam. She rarely spoke without yelling.

Wilfong addressed the stranger seated next to him: "I have 25 million dollars in the bank."

The man, suspecting that Wilfong was unbalanced, only stared at the field uncomfortably.

"I said, I have 25 million dollars in the bank. I would be willing to give it away if I could find a recipient who fears the Second Coming of our Lord, coming as He is on clouds of glory and lightning and thunder."

Again, the man did not respond; he was interested in the football game. Besides which, Wilfong made him uneasy. Weingrad assumed the man was deaf: "Hey Grizelda, there's a man here who is deaf."

Then Howard (Skip) Leslie threw a long, long pass whose spiral was so tight and pure it was a thing of beauty. It sailed many, many yards over the heads of offenders and defenders alike until it bounced harmlessly onto the ground in the end zone.

Grizelda bellowed, "*Mein Gott*! Could you just lookit der arm?!"

Back in the huddle, Robin Snook was still pleading, "Just one more try, Skip. Just one more chance with no blocking."

Howard Leslie was pleased to hear Robin call him by his nickname, but he had heard the *oohs* and *aahs* of the crowd in response to his long spiral pass. He decided he would throw another long, incomplete spiral, only this time even higher and farther.

*

In order to fulfill a new student obligation, Vano was expected to meet with his advisor early in the semester. The office of his advisor, Chaplain Johansen, was located on the third floor of the campus's oldest edifice, the previous administration building. The building was due for razing as soon as funds became available. Most of the floor where the chaplain's office was housed was being used for storage.

Chaplain Johansen was thin and pale. When Vano

found him, he was perusing a catalogue of evangelists. "I get these catalogues free because of my office," he informed Vano.

A period of silence lasted 15 seconds before the chaplain finally said, "I wonder if you might like to look at the catalogue?"

"I would enjoy looking at it," Vano answered.

Chaplain Johansen handed it over, and Vano began thumbing pages. It had the shiny paper stock of a mail order catalogue. There were pictures of evangelists on each page. Along with each picture, there was a paragraph describing the background and style of the evangelist. There was an easy-order blank in the back of the catalogue, so you could pick the preacher of your choice by simply filling out the form and mailing it in.

Vano read the page which delineated the qualifications of Billy Joe Jim Bob of Tupelo, Mississippi. There was a $20 rebate coupon which you could tear out and mail in if you ordered Billy Joe Jim Bob before October 31. "I never saw a catalogue like this before," said Vano.

"I daresay most people haven't," replied Chaplain Johansen. "You wouldn't think it possible to order an evangelist from a catalogue, the way you might order a washing machine from Sears. But there is the proof, right in front of you." He giggled nervously.

Vano returned the catalogue to the chaplain. After another protracted silence, Johansen said, "I receive a great deal of pleasure from mimeographing. I have my own mimeograph machine."

"That's nice."

The chaplain showed Vano a sheet of plain white paper with a single question printed near the center of the page: *If a deaf moose bellows in the forest, but only a snail is there to hear it, does the bellowing moose in fact make any sound?*

"Where are the rest of the questions?" Vano wanted to know.

"That's the whole test, just the one question. That's how Oboe likes his tests. He says they're easier to grade that way."

"I know who Oboe Meel is. He's my philosophy teacher."

"Oh my," fussed Chaplain Johansen, "Maybe I shouldn't have shown you the test. But he's the only one who brings me mimeo work these days of computers and laser printers. It used to be that lots of people did."

Vano made no response. He was in deep.

The chaplain said, "I can't remember why you're here. Sometimes I have problems with my memory."

"It's a requirement because you're my advisor."

"Yes of course, now I remember. Your roommate called me on the phone, by the way. He said you haven't been yourself lately."

By the time Vano was able to answer, he said, "I've been myself only more so. I go deeper in. Sometimes Arnold gets concerned about me, but he really doesn't need to."

"You go deeper in? When your roommate called, he kept asking me if there was a tap on my phone."

Vano smiled, but didn't answer.

The chaplain continued, "Your roommate said something to me about an atomic telephone. He said if I had an atomic telephone, no one could eavesdrop on my conversations."

"That sounds like Arnold," said Vano.

"Arnold believes you have a spiritual connection of some sort. What does he mean by that?"

It was a long, long time before Vano's answer came.

64

"Maybe spiritual connection is a good way of putting it. As good as any."

"I don't mean to pry," Chaplain Johansen said, "But I would very much enjoy hearing about a thing like that."

"Of course," said Vano. Speaking very slowly, from deep in, Vano proceeded with a summary. He explained to the chaplain about the phenomenon of *hooommm*. He summarized his visit with the particle people. He reviewed the basic tension between the particle mode and the ego mode. It did not occur to him to say anything about baseball or the blow to the head he suffered from Jose Canseco's bat. It seemed odd to share it all for the first time, but not uncomfortable. The chaplain was a good listener.

"My, but this is fascinating," said Chaplain Johansen, upon the completion of the summary. "I hope you don't mind that I'm taking notes."

"Taking notes is very nice."

"Is there more to tell?"

After some moments Vano replied, "There's no more to tell. There is more to learn, but I haven't learned it yet. The particle people said they hoped that some day my understanding might be complete."

The chaplain skimmed the notes he had taken. "I hope you don't mind my saying so," he said, "but this is almost like a sort of celestial pantheism."

Vano Lucas had read some material about pantheism, but didn't understand it. He told Johansen, "I don't mind your saying so."

Another lengthy silence ensued until finally, Vano excused himself and left.

After Vano's departure, Johansen reread his notes before he was able to extrapolate what he perceived to be the essence. He typed a stencil and fitted it to the drum of his mimeograph machine. As soon as he cranked out the first copy, he examined it closely:

> ***The Lord God is alive and well***
> ***And floating through particle dust.***

The chaplain smiled. There were no typographical errors, and the entire message was well centered on the page. He signed his name in mimeo ink, then ran off two thousand copies.

Since he had nothing else to do, he hand-delivered large stacks of the memo to the student union, the athletic complex, Coleman Hall, the library, the administration building, and three other academic buildings. Then Chaplain Johansen went home with a strong sense of accomplishment.

The next morning, President Reggie Rose saw the memo for the first time. He asked Mrs. Askew, "What does this mean?"

"I have no idea. Who is Chaplain Johansen?"

"Don't ask me," snapped Reggie Rose. "He must be listed in the staff directory. Look him up and get him over here."

Reggie went into his office, closed the door, sank into his comfortable chair, belched twice, and experienced a keen wave of heartburn. For breakfast, Bertie Kerfoot had fixed him some stale pizza and room temperature Dr. Pepper.

In ten minutes, Chaplain Johansen arrived. "I remember you," Reggie informed him gruffly.

"I keep a low profile," admitted the chaplain. His skin was very white and his demeanor timid. He wore a clerical collar. He had thin white hands which he kept clasped over his stomach.

"Don't stand there, Man, sit down." Reggie instructed him.

Chaplain Johansen sat down. He wore a charcoal gray crewneck sweater and shiny pleated pants. Around his neck hung a string of rosary beads and a Celtic cross. He fiddled nervously with the beads.

Taking note of this, Reggie asked, "Are you Catholic?"

"You know, that's the funny thing," replied the chaplain. "I've been involved in this ecumenical *milieu* for so long, I just can't remember. I can't remember which denomination I'm associated with." Saying this, Johansen laughed a long and nervous laugh.

Reggie Rose couldn't imagine what was funny. *What kind of idiot am I dealing with here*? he asked himself. "What are your beliefs then, Man?"

"You know the truth, I can't remember that, either. That's funny, too." Chaplain Johansen giggled some more.

What little patience Reggie had was gone. He pounded his desk, got very serious, and stood up to pace. He paced around his desk first this way, then the other. As he paced, he waved a copy of Johansen's memo. "I want to know the meaning of this," he demanded. "What's your authority for this?"

"I thought it might be inspirational. Maybe I was a bit too hasty. Sometimes I run out of things to do. I get a great deal of pleasure from mimeographing, but nobody brings me any work except Oboe Meel."

What is this chaplain babbling about? Reggie wondered. Before he could wonder too long, he felt another wave of heartburn. "Never mind all that," he told Johansen. "If you can excuse me for a moment, I'll be right back." He walked across to Mrs. Askew's office.

He asked her, "Is there anything in the trustees' report about getting more godly?"

Mrs. Askew had to think for a minute. She twiddled her glasses. "I remember one trustee saying we don't have any soul."

"That's close enough for me," said Reggie. Maybe this chaplain was on to something. Maybe getting back to God and stuff like that would get the college on the right track. When he returned to his office he told Chaplain Johansen: "You have my full support; keep up the good work."

"You mean I can run more copies?"

"Absolutely. The sky's the limit as far as I'm concerned."

Chaplain Johansen thanked him and left. It was now Reggie Rose's turn to feel the strong sense of accomplishment.

*

The Saturday night bash at Professor Revuelto's lakeside home was an invitation-only affair. Vano and Arnold were placed at the scene by the magic carpet effect of Robin Snook's coattails. He seemed to carry them along like production extras.

Vano's identity was a known factor to a few people, particularly those individuals recruited by Coach Radulski to act as his agents. It was their thankless task to try and influence him to return to the diamond. For the most part, though, Vano dwelled in campus anonymity, and so it was at this party.

There were kegs aplenty next to the strident rock'n'

roll band playing on the spacious deck. Japanese lanterns lighted the way clear to the beach front, where a few people were swimming in spite of the chill night air. Some of the swimmers wore swim suits, while others were wearing nothing.

Mary Thorne was standing at the threshold of the pier, drinking a raspberry wine cooler and talking with a *Playboy* photographer named Dickie Yen. Yen was explaining to her that he was on assignment to do a pictorial called *The Girls of Idaho*.

"This isn't Idaho," Mary pointed out to him. "I'd say you took a wrong turn somewhere."

"Okay, so I'm cheating just a bit. I couldn't find enough beautiful women in Idaho. When I found one who was willing to take her clothes off for a shoot, she usually looked like a professional field hockey player."

"Oh right. Like there's such a thing as professional field hockey."

"I guess you've got me there."

Mary Thorne was a 22 year old senior, majoring in home economics. Her ample chest, which measured out at 38D, was sculpted in high relief by her 24 inch waist. She was five feet, nine inches tall, and weighed 130 pounds. She had lustrous dark hair with a trace of coppery auburn tint. Her features were fine and regular, but no more so than her teeth.

Mary usually wore the provocative kind of clothing which underscored the contours of her voluptuous figure. She was a woman of rare beauty, a fact she understood clearly. She enjoyed knowing how men lusted after her because, as Camille Paglia put it, that was power. Mary enjoyed power as much as the next person.

There was almost no man on campus who could be indifferent in her presence, or maintain his hormonal equilibrium. Even the impervious Oboe Meel usually broke a sweat along his upper lip.

Dickie Yen told Mary, "You'll be a centerfold, I can practically guarantee that. You're the most beautiful woman I've ever seen." Dickie was sincere in this observation, and he had seen many, many beautiful women.

"A centerfold?" asked Mary. "Are you serious?"

"I've never been more serious. Trust me on this."

"Gee, now I don't know," said Mary.

"It pays fifty thousand dollars."

This piece of information gave Mary further pause. Now she had to think. She thought, *my body is so beautiful I should share it with the world at large.* Then she thought, *fifty thousand is a lot of money.* She thought some more: *If I pose for the centerfold, a lot of scumbags will see it; they will pin my picture up on the wall and pound off while they look at it.* Then she couldn't help thinking again, *fifty thou is a lot of money.*

It was fatiguing to work through these difficult thoughts. Mary turned to Dickie Yen and asked, "Would Kowalski see it?"

Naturally, Yen had no ready answer for this question. "Who is Kowalski and would he see what?"

"He's an animal, he's subhuman, he's a shit, he's a scumbag, he's--"

"Okay, okay, I get the picture," Yen interrupted. "He's someone on this campus, right?"

"Right. If I had my picture taken with no clothes on, would Kowalski get to see it?"

"Well, I suppose so. I don't know what would stop him."

"Then no."

"Then no?"

"Then no. If he gets to see it, then no picture."

"You're telling me you would turn down fifty thousand dollars because Kowalski would see the picture?"

"Now you understand."

For nearly 20 minutes, Dickie Yen tried to argue Mary out of this position, but she would not be dissuaded. He even followed her clear to the deck, where she left him standing by himself.

Arnold Beeker had found his way to Professor Revuelto's lower-level den, where he was playing *Super Mario* on a computer. Vano was alone in Revuelto's library, sipping a beer and inspecting the spines of the professor's many books. When he came to the leather-bound volumes, he breathed deeply their aroma and let his fingers travel the ridges. A junior named Rita Lieberman approached him to strike up a conversation. Rita wanted to know how he got an invitation to the party.

It took a while to find an answer. In addition to the fact he was deep in, Vano didn't know this person. "I don't think I got an invitation," he finally admitted.

"If you didn't get one, why are you here?"

"I guess I came with Robin."

"Like I'm sure I know what that's supposed to mean." said Rita. "I got invited this afternoon because I helped Professor Revuelto unload some Aztec statues. Every statue is an Aztec warrior with a hard-on. He got the statues on his trip to Guatemala. They look about a thousand years old, but I happen to know they're manufactured in this factory in San Diego. Either that, or they're made in Korea. Do you know what I'm saying to you?"

When he was able to answer, Vano replied, "I think you're saying that the statues aren't authentic."

"Would you mind speeding up a little bit with the answers? I'll tell you one thing, though, every one of the statues has about a nine inch schwantz. I wonder if the Aztecs were really hung like that."

Vano wondered if he was supposed to provide some sort of answer, but it didn't matter. Rita continued, "I'm a Jewish princess."

"That's nice," said Vano.

"I have a powerful sexual appetite," she added.

"That's nice too."

"Do you know what a Jewish princess is?"

"No, I don't."

Rita Lieberman proceeded to tell him. "A Jewish princess has a doting father. In his eyes, she can do no wrong, so he loves to spoil her with attention and gifts. My father has given me lots of expensive gifts. I drive a red Corvette which he gave me last spring."

"I see." Vano took a closer look at Rita. She was tall and awkward and gawky. Her hands, wrists, elbows, knees, and ankles were large and bony. Her frizzy hair was carrot colored. She had buck teeth. Vano concluded you didn't have to be beautiful to become a Jewish princess.

Rita continued, "Sex is one thing I can't seem to get enough of. The truth is, I wouldn't mind having one of Revuelto's statues in my apartment. I mean, we're talking about a nine inch stiff which never goes down. In a few years, I plan to write a best-selling book about campus sex. The title of the book is going to be, *How to Seduce a College Man and Make him your Slave."*

Vano was so deep in that a pause of more than five seconds yawned in advance of his response. "I like to read," he said. "Writing must be nice too."

"Hey, didn't I tell you to speed up with the answers? The one thing that really pisses me off is beautiful women who can get all the men they want, without any effort. Mary Thorne is the worst. She's so beautiful that men practically cream their jeans whenever she's in the neighborhood. I resent the hell out of her."

Vano didn't know who Mary Thorne was, but he tried a suggestion: "Maybe Mary Thorne could help you write your book."

"Are you out of your gourd?? Look, I can't stand the bitch; I'm not about to do her any favors."

Vano receded down his inscape into deeper *hooommm*. "It was just a suggestion."

"Yeah, well it's a suggestion that sucks. To get back to the bitch herself, the only flaws on Mary Thorne's body are the ones I put there, I'm proud to say. I stabbed her in the back three times with my nail file. She's got these little scars, about half an inch long, between her shoulder blades."

Vano asked if he could see the nail file, and Rita was happy to comply. She took it from her purse. It was six inches long, and made of heavier gauge steel than a conventional nail file. Its point was razor sharp. "I keep it sharpened on a grinding wheel," Rita explained.

Vano asked if it was really necessary to stab Mary with it.

Rita raised her voice, "Of *course* it's necessary! I *told* you, I *hate* her. Didn't I tell you that?"

In his zone, Vano was not perturbable. He had nothing to say, but his bland and pleasant smile was fixed. It was the visage his father often urged him to wipe off his face.

"Look," Rita explained. "In a way, I'm doing Mary Thorne a favor. Because of her looks, everything is too easy for her. She needs to know that she can expect problems in life, the same as everyone else. That's just reality."

Vano said, "I didn't think of it like that."

Then Rita changed the subject. "On the night of our senior prom, I gang fucked four guys in a Mercedes on the high desert near Palmdale. Has anything remarkable ever happened to you?"

"I don't know," said Vano. He thought of the night when he and Sister Cecilia made love, and wondered if Rita Lieberman would enjoy hearing about that. Then there was getting hit in the head by Jose Canseco's bat. That was surely remarkable, by almost any standard.

"Oh, there must be something," Rita insisted.

Vano went deeper in before he said, "We were on our senior class trip at Magic Mountain. I was standing under the sky chute when a girl fell out of her harness. She fell all the way down and landed on the blacktop real close to me. She was wearing a white blouse and a pair of blue shorts. Her body was just busted all up. There was blood and guts all over, like a run-over possum on the road."

"Very gross, I'm sure," said Rita. "I'll tell you what: you're not much of a talker, but you have a good body. How about if you and I get it on?"

Vano was pretty sure she was talking about sex. "I guess it would be okay," he said.

"I'll go get the Vette," Rita told him. "It's going to take me a few minutes, I had to park over by the marina. Just wait right here till I get back."

"That sounds nice," said Vano. He was left alone to ponder whether having sex with Rita Lieberman would provide any substantial pleasure, when Mary Thorne approached him to ask for a light. She had a cigarette between her lips.

"No, I'm sorry, I don't have one," said Vano.

She put the cigarette away in her purse. "It's just as well, I need to cut back. What I really ought to do is quit."

Vano didn't know this person either, but the answer

seemed simple enough. "It would be good for you to quit. Smoking is bad for your health."

"You're agreeable, aren't you? Do I know you?"

Agreeable, thought Vano. *That word again.* He said, "I don't think we know each other."

Mary was still seething about Kowalski, even though he would never see the pictures which would never be taken. It was the *principle* of the thing. "Let me ask you something," she said to Vano. "Why are men the way they are?"

The question was too hard. Vano listened serenely to his own primary resonance.

"May I have a sip of your beer?"

This was easier. "Of course," he said, handing her the can.

Before she continued, she took two or three swallows. "Let me put it to you this way. If it's not guys like Dickie Yen who want you naked for taking pictures, it's horny vermin like Kowalski looking to get their rocks off. Am I right?"

Even though Vano was unfamiliar with the two names, by listening to her words while looking at her physical beauty, Vano was able to get the drift. Even so, the answer was a long time coming. "I think you're saying men don't treat you with respect. They just want to use you for pleasure."

"That's it exactly."

"It makes you a sex object rather than a person."

"I couldn't say it any better myself. You really are agreeable, aren't you?"

"I guess I am," he admitted. "I'm getting so used to being called it, I can't think of any reason why agreeable wouldn't be appropriate."

"I bet you treat women with respect."

After five seconds Vano replied, "I guess I do, but I'm pretty sure I used to be the other way."

"That's hard to believe. You know what? I could get *heat* for you."

"That's nice."

"Do you know what I'm saying?"

"No I don't."

"Compared to Kowalski, you're the other end of the spectrum. I *am* getting heat for you."

Vano wondered what to say, but the agenda was all Mary's now. She looked at him with eyes that glittered. "It's been a long time. Why don't you follow me into the bedroom?"

"Okay, sure."

She took Vano into the bedroom, closed the door, switched on the dresser lamp, and turned down the bedspread. Vano wondered if he was betraying Rita Lieberman, but only briefly.

Mary began taking off her clothes. While doing so, she delivered an *apologia*: "I've never been promiscuous in my life, but every once in a while I get a truly desperate need for a particular man. My hormones go into overdrive and all my juices start to flow. I call it *getting heat*."

Vano's mouth was open, watching as she removed her brassiere. Mary continued by saying, "There's no way I can explain it. I never know how long the heat will last when it comes. When I was a sophomore, it was Sydney Gibbs. He's an electrician for god's sake, but it was his long blond hair that touched it off. It lasted about six weeks, then it was over. I've been celibate ever since then. That's too long."

By this time, she was completely nude. She stood facing Vano with her feet apart and her hands on hips. "I'm getting heat. *Now* do you understand?"

Vano's beleaguered *hooommm* roiled and timbred orange and active, but he was like a desperate swimmer treading water to stay afloat. Nevertheless, he sported a hard-on the texture of a brick. "Yes I do understand," he said.

Mary Thorne undressed him rapidly, climbed on top so as to straddle him, then slipped him inside. It didn't take long, but just before he shot his wad, face-to-face with the sway of her remarkable breasts, Vano threatened to break the surface. So intense was his state of disorientation, so tenuous his deep in lodging, that he even felt a brief urge to throw his slider again.

But by the time he squeezed off the last and feeblest contraction, he was receding down again, down and deeper down where the vibes were firm to shimmer him in the resonance like a perpetual gong.

When they were finished, they lay side by side. "I might get heat for you again," said Mary.

Since he was so way down deep, it took even longer than usual. "That would be nice," he finally responded.

"Is that all you can say?"

"It would be *very* nice."

Mary Thorne was more than a little annoyed. "Don't you know who I am?" She got out one of her cigarettes, forgetting in her moment of pique that there was no lighter. She left it between her lips anyway. "Do you realize how many guys would give their left nut to be where you are right now?"

"No, I guess I don't."

"Are you always this agreeable?"

Vano was watching the bobbing, unlit cigarette. "Yes, I guess I am."

"I think you are. I could definitely get *heat* for you again."

"That would be very nice."

Chapter Four

It was not a congenial beginning to Reggie Rose's day. For breakfast, Bertie Kerfoot served him a cold jar of pig's knuckles, one week old, with a head cheese spread. She gave him a partial bottle of Dr. Pepper.

While he nibbled with no enthusiasm, Bertie embroidered the experience by smoking her cigarette in his direction and disclosing the pathological condition of her sister's hemorrhoids in much detail. "I'm sure it's going to come to surgery," she said. "I may have to go and visit her."

This would put her behind the wheel. "Why don't you have a drink?" suggested Reggie. "Maybe a few fingers of J&B would relieve some of your stress." If she had a few drinks, she might steer herself over the edge on one of the canyon roads. Reggie visualized Bertie's car in a freefall, plummeting to a fiery crash. He could almost hear the headlines. *Tape at eleven.*

Bertie said, "I sure hope they use that new technique where they tie those little devils off instead of doing the actual cutting."

Reggie dropped his fork and stood up. He could stand no more. He decided to hie himself to the office and try his luck with Mrs. Askew. He told Bertie, "I'd like to stay here and discuss this with you, there's so much work to be done. You have no idea."

As soon as he got to the office, he dealt with Mrs.

Askew aggressively: "Get that coach on the phone, that Washinski, that whatsisname."

"You mean Coach Radulski."

"That's the one. I want to know about that pitcher. I want to find out when we can expect the revenue to come pouring in."

Mrs. Askew informed him that there was a new memo from the trustees regarding curriculum development. "According to the memo, it's imperative," she said. "It has to become a priority."

Reggie thought of the pig's knuckles and listened to his stomach churn. "I'm going to ferret out the academic dean," he declared. "Curriculum development ought to be his sphere."

"Good luck," Mrs. Askew told him.

"Thank you." As soon as he closed his office door, Reggie began to pace. *If we don't do something soon in curriculum development, we will be in serious trouble--the trustees' report is quite explicit on that point.*

This thought was nonplussing in the extreme. He sat down hard in his swivel chair. He thought, *what the hell am I supposed to do about curriculum development?* And then he thought, *what would be the perfect crime to hasten Bertie Kerfoot's demise?*

He stood up to resume his pacing. This led him in the direction of a more comforting thought: *I deserve a decent breakfast. Things like curriculum development will have to wait.*

Mrs. Askew entered to inform him that Coach Radulski was not in his office.

"Where is he, then?"

"His secretary thinks he might be out on the playing field."

"At eight in the morning? Is there a phone there?"

"No, no phone. You could walk over to the field and check. It's not far."

"Don't be silly, I'm the president. Just keep trying his office."

Then Reggie went to the union, where he had orange juice, a very nice onion and green pepper omelette, and hot coffee. He ate ever so slowly so as to relish every mouthful of this delicious repast. On his table was a matchbook. While he chewed, he read the backside of its cover:

Learn astrology! Delight your friends!
Earn big bucks at home, charting!

President Rose put the matchbook in his pocket. Astrology was big nowadays. He ordered more coffee and prepared to linger over it, but then Professor Revuelto came barging in. Reggie winced. He feared Revuelto would want to join him, but as luck would have it, the beefy Cuban spotted a table of students. Just after dropping his briefcase noisily, Revuelto twirled out of his paisley neck scarf. He threw his arms wide to proclaim: "My dear ones! Let us come together!"

The students to whom he spoke were playing cards in close proximity to Reggie's table. They mumbled and grumbled and shoved around reluctantly to make room for Revuelto to sit down.

Finding his seat, Revuelto clapped a few of the students on the back, then loudly ordered two fried eggs, sausage links, hash browns, four pieces of toast, and orange juice. He began telling the students all about some of his close calls with Venezuelan officials and underworld figures. Very little of what he told them was factual.

Then the breakfast came. Revuelto began devouring the eggs and toast aggressively, in doubled-up forkfuls.

Perspiration beaded on his forehead and ran in little rivulets down his chubby, swarthy face. The uncooked white of the eggs dribbled in cloudy streams through his chin whiskers. Egg yolk stuck in his mustache. Revuelto gobbled on.

Seated next to him was Rita Lieberman. She stared at the spectacle of Revuelto with his eggs and toast and said, "Oh my god."

Revuelto looked at her briefly, then threw back his head to laugh savagely. Small fragments of his breakfast erupted from his mouth like spray.

"Oh my god," Rita repeated herself. She moved her chair to a safer distance.

Reggie Rose had to wonder by this time whether this breakfast experience was significantly better than his earlier one with Bertie. After he paid his bill, he left quickly.

He found Oboe Meel basking on the quad with two maintenance men and a nondescript student of passive body language. He sat down just in time to hear Sydney Gibbs ask Oboe, "How many kids do you have, Oboe?"

"Sixteen. I have sixteen children."

"Why so many?"

Oboe did not find this question impertinent. He said, "I will be happy to tell you."

Reggie Rose turned instantly glum, for he knew this answer would be lengthy in the extreme.

Oboe began by saying, "There is in every man a longing for recognition which endures. The idea of a lasting effect. Some people call this immortality, and link it in some fashion with a belief in God and/or the hereafter."

He continued, "I too have such a longing. I too want to have an impact on the world. My way of doing this is by creating as many little Meels as possible, and sending them out into the world. In other words, my offspring are my lasting effect."

"Well, I always wanted to know," said Sydney Gibbs. "Thanks a lot for telling me."

"Did you ever hear of a thing called birth control?" asked Billy Byrd, the second maintenance man.

But as Oboe was not finished, he found it convenient to ignore both remarks. "It isn't only that I have sired 16 children. Oh no. I have sired 16 *consuming* children. Most all of my offspring have reached adulthood; only one is still in her teens. All the children are voracious consumers. They all own at least one full-sized car which consumes large quantities of fuel. They all have closets full of clothes. They have computers and video games and televisions and VCRs. They have audio tapes, video tapes, and CDs. They use many cans, bottles, plastic, and paper products."

"Well, thanks again for telling me."

Oboe went on, "Having 16 children would account for some impact on the world, I suppose, but having 16 consuming children! Think of the impact on the world's resources! Think of the drain on forests and petroleum products and landfills and even the sea itself! In this way, do you see, I am achieving a lasting effect."

Oboe paused long enough to take several deep breaths. He took out his red bandanna and began wiping his forehead. Leaping to their feet, Sydney Gibbs and Billy Byrd seized the opportunity to excuse themselves. Vano Lucas, the silent student, did not move or speak; he took no notice of the two maintenance men in motion.

Reggie had taken the matchbook absently from his pocket. He worried it from one hand to the other. Having endured Meel's excruciating verbal tome, he had little patience: "See here, Meel, there's a great deal of work to be done in curriculum development."

Oboe's eyes were closed. "Does this sound like a topic which will excite my interest?"

"If we don't do something soon in curriculum development, we will be in serious trouble."

"What I know about curriculum development would probably not fill a thimble. What I care about it would be considerably less."

"The trustees' report is quite specific on this point," persisted Reggie.

Oboe responded with a rhetorical question: "Have I not told you on prior occasions that your trustees' report is a fiction?"

Reggie fumed inwardly, but sighed out loud. His eyes traveled impatiently across the printing on the matchbook in his hand. A thought came to him: "See here, Meel, what about astrology?"

Oboe opened his eyes long enough to ask, "What about it?"

"I'm asking you for your opinion on astrology."

He closed his eyes again. "There are those who find it fascinating. For example, the lady who scavenges the aluminum cans from the dumpsters in our neighborhood."

Reggie stood up abruptly. He felt his energy returning. "Meel, I have to say I find your remarks encouraging. I say, let's consider that this matter is now under advisement."

"If that's what you say, I am not wont to quarrel with it."

Vano was so deep in it didn't occur to him that this was an odd sort of exchange.

Reggie left in higher spirits. He made his way directly to Mrs. Askew's desk. "Do we offer any courses in astrology, Mrs. Askew?"

"I doubt it."

"What do you think of astrology, if you don't mind my asking?"

"Personally, I would never set foot out of the house without first consulting my horoscope."

Reggie found her remark even more encouraging than Oboe Meel's. He inquired, "Mrs. Askew, what is it exactly that the trustees' report says about our curriculum?"

She had to pause a few moments while she chewed her pencil. "Well, for one thing, it says we need to set our sights higher."

"That's good enough for me," said Reggie. "You can't set your sights much higher than the stars in the heavens."

He went to his office where he collapsed in the swivel chair. Tired though he was, he felt a strong sense of accomplishment. First (through his encounter with Chaplain Johansen), he had struck the initiative to move the campus in the direction of godliness. Now, he was about to take the lead in curriculum development.

*

It was on a Thursday afternoon when Mary Thorne made her way up to the third floor of Vano's dorm. Then she made her way to Vano's room. This was against policy, as these were not designated visiting hours, but when Mary was *getting heat,* she didn't let much of anything stand in her way.

Robin Snook was at football practice, but Arnold Beeker was seated at his desk, working on a calculus template on his computer screen. Mary said to Arnold, "Get lost."

Arnold could tell by her demeanor that this wasn't the time to proclaim his rights. He left. As soon as he was gone, Mary closed the door behind him. She embraced Vano savagely, then began rapidly removing his clothes.

They made love passionately (at least for her part) on his bed in a feverish congress which lasted the better part of 20 minutes. Then Mary sat on the edge of the bed and smoked a cigarette, yet another policy violation. While doing this she informed him, "Coach Radulski keeps calling me. He wants me to influence you to pitch baseball."

This information didn't surprise Vano, nor did it disturb the comfortable resonance of his zone.

"He's an alkie," said Mary. "I bet you didn't know that."

"I think I did know that," Vano replied.

"He wants me to manipulate you."

When Vano had the reply he wanted, he said, "I used to be a pitcher. I'm pretty sure I was very good. What did you say to him?"

"I told him to kiss off. I don't manipulate, I get heat." She dropped her cigarette into a waiting Mountain Dew can and listened to the *ssizzz*. Then she changed the subject. "It's a burden to have a body this beautiful. I bet you never thought of that, did you?"

"I'm pretty sure I never have, Mary."

"A little faster, huh? The point is, when you have a body this beautiful you have to take care of every part. Just take my feet for instance. If I'm going to wear sandals, which I often do, I have to make sure my feet are beautiful. How many people have to deal with *that* ??"

Vano tried to think about it briefly, but couldn't get anywhere.

Mary went on, "You have no idea the work that goes into it. Your feet have to be tan on top. They don't have to be tan on the bottom, feet are the one place where it's okay to have a tan line. Your feet always have to be real clean and well manicured; sloppy toenails are really gross. *Really* gross. Then if you want to put nail polish on your toenails, it has to be just the right shade. I had this nice beige shade once in the spring, but as soon as my feet got tan, the shade didn't work at all. The color was too close to the color of my skin. Are you listening to me?"

"It's a real interesting viewpoint," said Vano. Even though Mary was still completely nude, his *hooommm* was firm and solid. He let his fingers travel gently the three white scars between her shoulder blades, but he was not sexually aroused by her physical beauty.

"I'm trying to explain something to you," Mary Thorne reminded him. "Do you understand what I'm saying to you?"

"What you said was very nice, Mary."

Mary sighed. It was a sigh of impatience. She stood up to begin putting on her bra. She lifted the lovely globes devoutly into the 38D *Cross Your Heart* Playtex Special. She said to Vano, "You're not very interesting, are you?"

New questions generated fog, so the answer didn't come quickly. "No, I guess not."

"You're real agreeable, though. Maybe you can't expect one with the other."

Vano had an idea: "You know what, Mary. I was thinking that you and I should have a date. All we ever do is have sex. If we went out on a date together, we might get to know each other better."

Mary Thorne put her blouse on. "Like I was saying, you're really not very interesting." Vano watched as she stepped into her white nylon bikini underpants. He couldn't help but wonder what would be the benefit of being interesting. To be polite, though, he asked, "What should I do about it?"

"Oh, I don't know. Change your major, maybe."

"I don't have a major," Vano informed her.

"Whatever." She was ready to leave now. "There's

never any telling how long the heat will last. You're very agreeable, but without being more interesting, I just can't say. Seeker can come back now."

"It's not Seeker, it's Beeker. Arnold Beeker."

"Whatever."

When Arnold returned, he had a splint on his right thumb. "What happened?" Vano asked.

"I just came from the health center," said Arnold. "It turns out I broke my thumb this morning."

Vano was geared up to apologize for kicking him out of the room at Mary's behest, but he decided this more current subject should be the agenda. "How did you break your thumb?" he inquired.

"I broke it in my computer," was the answer.

"You broke your thumb in your computer?"

"Yes, yes, if you have to know. I broke it in the printer."

Vano wondered if this might be the only case on record of a broken thumb by way of an Epson, but it would surely be embarrassing to ask such a question out loud. "I'm sorry," he said, "that you were kicked out of the room when Mary came. It's not fair."

Arnold was pouting just the same. "You think I haven't been treated this way my whole life?"

After Vano apologized a second time, he said, "Maybe you and I should go to the union. I'll buy your supper."

"The cafeteria meals are already paid for with our meal tickets, Vano."

After a lengthy delay, Vano said, "I'm pretty sure that was my attempt at humor."

"Ha ha," Arnold said.

On the way, they stopped at the union book store. It was Arnold's mission to seek out the latest installment of

New Age Chronicles, while Vano was content to simply browse. The target of this browsing was the large rack of popular paperbacks near the store's entrance. Some of the books, the kind that might be found in a drug store or discount house, were currently popular. Others had a more traditional popularity.

Vano's eyes moved from cover to cover:

> *The Jane Fonda Workout Book*
> *Chariots of the Gods*
> *Thin Thighs in 30 Days*
> *Buns of Steel*
> *The Late, Great Planet Earth*
> *Why Not You, Why Not Now?*
> *Looking Out for Number One*
> *Raquel's Guide to Beauty*
> *Tough Times Never Last, but Tough People Do*
> *You Are Worth It*
> *How to Pick up Girls*

There were more books on the rack, but suddenly Vano felt like the whole store was vibrating. It shimmered, taking his breath away. The titles of the books seemed to melt together while a fiery orange aura flared and consumed the rack. Vano was plunging deeper in than he'd ever gone before, at least while in a state of consciousness.

His head was swimming. He had to go to one knee to assure his own balance. The deafening roar was like a high-speed train blasting through a subway station. The only thing Vano could compare it to was his ballistic trip through the zone of the particle people on his way out of the coma.

The book store manager, who had noticed his plight, was offering him a chair. "You look a little pekid, young man, maybe you'd better sit down." But this book store manager, speaking through the dull roar, seemed so far away.

"Did I lose consciousness?" Vano asked.

"There's no need to yell. We're right here. I don't think you lost consciousness, but you look a little green around the gills. If you'll sit down, I'll fetch you a glass of water."

Arnold helped him into the molded plastic chair while the manager went to get the water. Arnold asked if he was okay, but the voice was too far away.

When the man returned, Vano said "Thank you. Do you have *Kon-Tiki*?"

"I'm sure we must have it. Here--drink a little of the water." Vano drank the whole glass. Then he inhaled and exhaled several times. He felt better.

By the time Vano got his tray and silverware, the roar had receded, and he found himself in a comfortable, modest range of firm resonance. He was able to navigate the cafeteria line smoothly, choosing a cheeseburger and fries.

When they sat down to eat, Arnold asked him once again if he was okay.

"I think I'll be fine."

With his mouth full of macaroni and cheese, Arnold announced, "I was over at the science building this morning. They're starting a spelunking club. I joined up."

Vano didn't answer. He saw how clumsy it was for his friend to manipulate his fork while wearing the thumb splint. He couldn't take his eyes off the seven ballpoint pens housed in Arnold's plastic pocket liner. *Hooommm.*

"The spelunking club is going to be keen times for everybody. The sponsor says there are real quality caves to explore between Stockton and Sacramento. I think you should join up too."

"Caves are nice," replied Vano. "I think they would be cool and resonant and peaceful."

"Is something the matter with you, Vano? Just listen to you. What are you staring at?"

He was too deep in to answer quickly. "I didn't realize I was staring."

"You're staring is what you're doing. What did you see in the book rack?"

This delay was even longer, nearly ten seconds. Then Vano said, "I think I saw the truth."

"The truth?"

"The truth about the books, I mean."

Arnold's mouth was full again. His words were garbled when he asked, "So what's with the truth about the books?"

First, a long deep breath. Then Vano explained, "The books in the rack are really the same book. Ostensibly, their subject matter may seem to be different--a more beautiful body, a religious vision, or a path to worldly success. But in fact, all these books exist to assist, reassure, or reinforce the vulnerable egos of people on earth. They are essentially the same book, because they have the same purpose."

Arnold Beeker swallowed his mouthful. "Vano, I've never heard you talk like this before."

Vano smiled. "I don't think I have either. It might be the particle people talking through me, and not me at all. It feels like the words come from somewhere else."

"The particle people? Did you say *particle people* ??"

Leaning back in his chair, Vano drank some of his Diet Coke. "I could tell you about this, if you'd like me to."

"Let's go, let's go. I *have* to hear it."

Speaking very slowly, from deep deep in, Vano proceeded to deliver the longest speech of his life. He explained to Arnold about the phenomenon of *hooommm*. He summarized his visit with the particle people, then reviewed the basic concepts of particle mode and ego mode. He described the physical appearance of the particle people in as much detail as he could remember.

Arnold received this body of information with his mouth open, in the shape of an O. "Vano, this puts me in total awe."

"They told me about something called *ultimate hooommm*. I'm not sure what it means, but they also told me that some day my understanding might be complete."

"*Ultimate hooommm??*" Arnold took off his new glasses and began to clean the lenses. He shook his head back and forth. "Vano, what can I say? This is *cosmic*! This is so fantastically cosmic that it truly humbles me." Arnold opened his looseleaf notebook and pushed aside his pie plate. He began asking questions so rapidly that Vano couldn't keep pace with his answers. One of the questions was about eternal life.

Vano explained, "The particle people already have eternal life. In their particle form they travel the universe at the speed of light. They don't experience the aging process. Sometimes they travel at tachyon speed, which is even faster than lightspeed."

Arnold Beeker felt like he had entered a holy sanctuary. "Vano, this is like you met God face to face."

Still deep in resonance, Vano delivered a quiet reply: "Confined by the ego mode, we are fond of imagining a huge man who lives in the sky. God is the name we give him. But in truth, there is just the universe expanding and contracting. There are the waves, and there are the particles."

"Can you please repeat that?" Arnold requested.

Vano repeated the statement.

"I've never heard you talk this way, Vano. I'm not sure I've heard anybody talk this way. You sound like a guru."

Vano tried to explain by saying, "That's why I think the particle people may be speaking through me. It doesn't feel like I'm choosing words, it feels more like I'm a receiver in a transmission."

Arnold closed his notebook and put his pen away. "No more right now, okay? Wait till we get back to the dorm. I'm going to have to plug this into the right program. I can tell you this much: I've thought up a lot of theories in my life, but nothing to compare to this."

"This isn't a theory, Arnold," was the answer, when it finally came. "This was an experience. Everything happened exactly as I told you."

Arnold glanced nervously at the people seated at the nearest table before he said, "Please keep your voice down."

Vano laughed. He tried to remember the last time he'd done so. "I don't make up theories, Arnold. I wouldn't know how to make up a theory."

In a hushed voice Arnold warned, "I'm only trying to give you the benefit of my experience. You need to be real careful where you talk about this; I've learned that lesson the hard way."

Vano was now entering the buzz of deeper resonance. He couldn't think of any reason not to share the particle people experience with anyone eager to hear about it. He wondered if he should tell Arnold how he had already shared some of it with Chaplain Johansen.

Arnold enlarged the scope of his warning with some detail: "I worked out this theory once about microwave ovens. I believe they were invented by the alchemists for the purpose of turning lead into gold. This proves that the microwave is not a new discovery at all. Microwaves have been around for hundreds of years."

Vano had some experience with microwaves, of course, but he didn't know what an alchemist might be. He smiled the pleasant smile.

Arnold concluded by saying, "I made the mistake of explaining my microwave theory in chemistry class. I'm just trying to warn you, you need to be real careful where you discuss things like particle people. I've been pantsed for spouting off theories that weren't half as cosmic as this."

Vano was still smiling. He wasn't hearing much of what Arnold said, as his friend's words were muffled by a *mezzoforte* roar. The cafeteria was gliding like ebb tide toward the orange horizon.

*

The day when Vano went in search of his philosophy teacher, Oboe Meel, he found him basking in the sun on a park bench on the quad. Sitting close at hand were the two maintenance men, Sydney Gibbs and Billy Byrd.

As soon as Vano took a spot near the end of the bench, he informed Oboe politely that he would like to do a book report on *In My Own Way* by Alan Watts. Oboe opened his eyes a tiny slit. He spat a firm arc of Red Man juice before he answered. "We don't do book reports in class." He might have added they were too much trouble to read, but decided against it.

"I think I might like to do it for extra credit."

"Extra credit? Extra credit means extra work."

Vano's *hooommm* was deep and firm. Oboe's slitted eyes made Vano think of a huge, inert reptile waiting for the sun to thin its blood. "I would be willing to do the extra work," he told the philosophy teacher.

"I don't mean extra work for you, I mean extra work

for me." Oboe opened his eyes a little wider before he said, "I remember Mr. Watts. There was a conference of some kind in a lodge at Mt. Tamalpais. That was in the late sixties, before your time."

Vano squinted against the sun to contemplate Meel's enormous silhouette. "I think my mother was one of his followers," he said.

Oboe's eyes flared a little wider. "What is it you're telling me?" he asked in his resonant voice.

"I'm not sure follower is the right word. I've seen pictures of my mother together with Alan Watts. She's dead now. Sister Cecilia showed me the pictures."

Oboe had no way of knowing who Sister Cecilia was. He asked Vano, "Is it possible then, that by studying the Watts autobiography you hope to feel bonded with your late mother?"

The reverberations which flared orange to scrim the horizon disturbed Vano's comfort zone. But not for long. "I never thought of it that way."

"Those who knew him claim he was promiscuous," said Oboe. "Are you aware of that?"

Promiscuous was a word that Mary sometimes used. "I'm just beginning my research," Vano answered.

"I can't imagine a more appropriate book report subject," were Meel's encouraging words. "How would an oral report suit you?"

"That would be nice."

"You could give the report to me right here on the bench."

"That would be nice."

"Excellent, then. Would you like to bask with us for a while?"

"It would be nice to sit for a while longer," said Vano. "I'm very deep in."

"Commendable indeed," Oboe endorsed. He hooked his thumbs securely again beneath his coverall straps. It was at this moment Kowalski joined the group. He took a seat next to Sydney Gibbs, without speaking.

Billy Byrd asked Oboe, "Oboe, hows come you like to come out here and sit with us? Hows come you don't sit in the union with the other teachers?"

Smiling broadly, Oboe closed his eyes. "Billy," he boomed, "I like to sit with you because you are real."

Billy, an electrician, had gray stubble on his chin. He replied, "Real, sheeit. There ain't much about me that's real, if you want the truth."

"You are real, Billy. Yours is a world of alternating current and direct current and watts and amps and terminals and relay switches. Such things are real."

"Sheeit," contested Billy Byrd. "I've got three plastic ducks on my wall at home in the den. Even the bricks on the wall are plastic. My wife still stuffs her bra with nylon stockings. You call any of that real?"

Oboe, however, was impenetrable. He only smiled the wider smile before he repeated firmly, "You are real."

Vano wondered if Oboe Meel was acquainted with *hooommm*.

The other electrician, Sydney , was much younger. But like Billy, he had spent most of his life on the farm before coming to work for college maintenance. Sydney introduced a negative note: "I'll tell you what's real. Life on the farm. Life on the fuckin' farm means bustin' your ass in the fields for about 16 hours a day."

Professor Meel concurred. "Farm work is very real."

Kowalski, who had joined the group to hear Sydney talk about Mary Thorne's body, decided that ought to be enough talk about farms. He said to Sydney, "Let's hear about Mary's tits again."

Sydney smiled. He was used to this, more or less, since making love to Mary two years earlier had made him a minor celebrity. He began by saying, "Mary has the nicest tits you've ever seen. They are big and round and white. Very white, with almost no sag."

"She has nice skin," murmured Kowalski.

Sydney confirmed it: "Nice skin big time. Very nice skin and very smooth. No blemishes. She has this golden tan everywhere except for her tits and her crotch. Her bush is just like the hair on her head, dark brown mostly only with a touch of red in it."

"Please, Sydney, I think I'm goin' to die," said Kowalski.

Sydney laughed out loud. "Hell, you're a big football hero, go find out for yourself." Then he took the cigarette from behind his ear and lit up.

Vano wondered if he should participate in this conversation. If the topic was going to be Mary Thorne's body, then he could possibly contribute something pertinent; perhaps the three tiny white scars between her shoulder blades. If reality was going to be the topic, then it might be salient for him to disclose something about *hooommm* or particle existence. Oboe and the other men, however, seemed to recede rapidly from foreground to background; Vano decided he was in too deep to participate; it would be nice to simply continue with the basking.

Billy Byrd was still thinking about life on the farm. He returned to that subject by observing, "The thing I hated most about the farm was you could never get all the painting done. I got my barn painted once, nice and white. *Very* white."

Oboe Meel approved: "White is nice for a barn."

"Nice, white skin," said Kowalski reverently.

Sydney Gibbs guffawed.

Billy continued, "But the shed was red. The barn was white, but the shed was red. I could never get it all just right, just the way I wanted it."

"Mhmmm," murmured Oboe, without opening his eyes.

"I mean, you always knew you wouldn't get the shed painted white until the next year, and the year after that there would be the crib starin' you in the face. If all that other stuff was white, then I figured the crib ought to be white."

"Uniformity is nice," said Oboe approvingly. "It tends to generate a feeling of control."

"By the time I got all those outbuildings painted white, the house would need it again, and then the barn, and so on and so on. I just never could get it all the way I wanted, all at the same time."

"It would be wise not to magnify the seriousness of this problem, though." Oboe reminded him.

Billy Byrd still had his teeth in it, however. "I'd say if I ever had a dream on the farm, that was it--to have the house, the barn, the crib, the shed, the tool shed, all painted white at exactly the same time. Even the dog house. Every one of them devils all painted white at the same time, all with a fresh, clean, white coat of paint."

Sydney said, "The first time I fucked Mary Thorne I mustuv come in about three strokes. Four strokes, tops."

Kowalski laughed.

"You didn't hear a thing I said, did you?" asked Billy Byrd.

"You was sayin' somethin' about barns. The first time I fucked her, I didn't hardly get my dick in before I shot my wad. It's a good thing there wasn't no delay, or I woulduv come all over her stomach."

"On that nice white skin," whispered Kowalski.

Billy Byrd stood up abruptly and cut himself a chew. "Sheeit," he said. "I'm goin' back to work."

It was moments after Billy left when Sydney and Kowalski did likewise. Oboe Meel turned to Vano to tell him, "Don't judge the boys by their conversation today. They usually function on a higher plane."

From deep in Vano said, "The conversation was very nice."

"You are skilled at basking," Oboe observed. "Please feel free to join us at any time."

"Thank you very much. That would be nice."

*

After lunch on Friday, Robin Snook and Vano were strolling the concourse in the student union when they passed a literature table. They removed the top sheet from a very tall stack of memos and read it together:

The Lord God is alive and well and moving through the particle dust of the universe.

Vano noticed Chaplain Johansen's signature at the bottom of the page.

"What the hell you suppose this means?" Robin asked.

Vano was feeling some oscillating flickers. "This sounds familiar," he said.

Robin picked up the entire stack of memos and said, "Did you ever do any leafleting?"

"No," answered Vano. "I never have."

"There's no practice on Fridays," said Robin. "Come with me, we'll do a little leafleting."

"Okay, sure."

They drove Robin's car. They headed for Main Street, which took them past the Kappa house. They spied several women sunning themselves on the lawn, including Mary Thorne.

"How'd you like to take a ride on Mary Thorne?" asked Robin.

"I've made love to Mary Thorne," Vano replied.

"Sure you have."

"She gets heat for me."

"Right."

"I'm going to make love to her again tonight."

"Sure," said Robin Snook. "That's the stuff."

They headed north out of town. "Where are we going?" asked Vano.

"To the Bakersfield Airport. We're going to do our leafleting the easy way."

"You mean you have an airplane?"

"I'm only taking lessons. All I have is a learner's license."

Vano smiled and said, "This sounds nice." Then he read one of the memos again. It was so reminiscent of the particle people visit that he went deep and deeper in, all the way to the airport.

When they got to the terminal, they found the flight instructor busy with paperwork. He told Robin, "I'm going to be tied up for a little while. You go on out to the plane and wait. I'll be along in a few minutes."

It was the wrong thing to say to Robin Snook. He and Vano walked to the plane, a blue and white single-engine Cirrus VK-30. "Hop in," said Robin. "I'll fire this baby up."

Shortly after they were belted in, Robin got ignition. He smiled at Vano and put his thumb up. In a matter of moments, they were taxiing down the runway at 70 miles per hour. "Shouldn't we wait for the instructor?" Vano asked him.

"Nah, I'm ready to solo."

Then they were off the ground. They hummed through the air and circled the campus a few times.

"Isn't there supposed to be a flight plan?" Vano asked.

"We'll think one up."

They flew high above the LaPanza range, north of San Luis Obispo. Robin seemed more than competent at the controls. Vano felt no trepidation, only a blissful sense of freedom, soaring out of time. It was a long flight, but Vano was oblivious to the clock, and even the limits of space seemed pushed back by the serpentine vista of mountain ranges merging with seacoast.

When Robin finally broke the silence he said, "We must be close to Monterey by now."

"I guess we've come a long way, then." Vano concluded.

"Yeah, farther than I thought. I have to watch the fuel. We better turn around, I couldn't fly this thing after dark." Saying this, Robin banked the plane away from the coast.

"This would be the flight plan, then." mumbled Vano.

"This would be it."

"What about the memos?"

"Oh yeah. Heave those babies on out."

"Sure," said Vano. He commenced to throw the memos out through the window of the plane in groups of 20 and 30. He wondered if some of them might end up in the ocean.

The memos dispersed rapidly, floating on the wind currents like confetti. Down, down, down they floated and fluttered. Most of the memos came to light on rooftops and streets and parking lots. One of the memos, on its downward spiral, darting this way and that, came to rest on the windshield of a 1956 Buick Roadmaster parked in the lot of the Southgate Mall near Salinas. A little corner of the memo tucked itself under the windshield wiper.

This massive Roadmaster was forest green and canary yellow. It was parked diagonally across three parking spaces. It belonged to Wilfong Weingrad, who had 25 million dollars in the bank. Wilfong had just patronized the Hobby Shop to purchase two small bottles of tempera paint. He needed it to paint moss on the viaducts which spanned the tracks of his electric train set.

Wilfong and his housekeeper, Grizelda, had seen the leaflets drop from the sky. They were standing next to the car when the leaflet settled securely into place on the windshield.

"This must be from the Lord," declared Wilfong.

Grizelda reached to remove the memo from the windshield, but Wilfong ordered, "Leave it alone! If this is something from the Lord, don't touch it!"

Grizelda shrugged. She got behind the wheel while Wilfong climbed into the back seat. Grizelda's view was partially obscured by the memo on the windshield, but this did not bother her substantially. She took a half-full bottle of Jim Beam from the glove box, unscrewed the top, then took a long, gurgling swallow. She capped the bottle, put it away, started the engine, bulled her way across the parking lot, and then swung aggressively into traffic.

She worked her way swervingly through 24 miles of rural blacktop and increasing elevation, until she reached the wooded hillside niche which protected the Weingrad estate. When she got to Wilfong's lane, she lurched the car to a rough stop in front of the mailbox. A large metal statue of a crusader, complete with chain-mail armor, held Wilfong's mailbox in the crook of its left arm. Another of Chaplain Johansen's memos was impaled on the tip of the crusader's sword.

"It's another one!" Wilfong shrieked. "It's got to be a sign!"

When they reached the huge house, they stumbled into the kitchen. Wilfong stumbled because he was old and decrepit, while Grizelda stumbled because she was intoxicated.

Weingrad found his way to the den, where there were 32 cuckoo clocks on the wall. They were all different sizes and shapes. Some were German, some were Swiss, and some were Mexican. One was made in Hong Kong and another in Korea. Wilfong sat at his desk and began opening drawers with his shaky fingers. He found his glasses, but it took a long time to wrap the thin wire frames around his ears. The glasses in place, he turned on the desk lamp so as to read the memos very carefully. He moved his lips as he went along.

Then all the cuckoo clocks went off at once and Wilfong nearly had a myocardial infarction. The clocks were never supposed to be wound, but Grizelda couldn't resist.

"Goddamit, woman, I've told you never to wind these clocks!" His heart was palpitating. After he pulled his hearing aide out, he stumbled into the kitchen. Grizelda was passed out face down on the table, but Weingrad was too preoccupied to notice. He announced to his housekeeper: "These people have the fear o' the Lord in 'em! Get 'em on the phone!"

Chapter Five

It was two weeks later when Vano's father came to get him. Vernon eased the Town Car to a halt directly in front of the dorm, in the red zone, got out of the car, and went straight inside. Mrs. Kuetemeyer, the R.A., badgered him all the way to the elevator about the parking violation, but he simply brushed her aside.

Vano wasn't in his room, but Vernon found him in the lounge. He came right to the point, and not gently: "Get your things packed; you're coming home for a while."

Since he was deep in, and since he wasn't expecting his father anyway, Vano had no response forthcoming.

"I said get your things packed. You're coming home for a while until we can get some of this stuff sorted out." Without waiting for a response, Vernon left to wait in the car.

Vano felt a perplexity which triggered a short-term flickering. He went to his room to begin packing his suitcase. Robin Snook wasn't there, but Arnold Beeker was. He asked Vano what he was doing.

"I'm packing my things. My father is outside in the car. He says he's taking me home for a few days."

"But why?"

"I'm not sure," said Vano, after an extended delay. He was finished packing his clothes, and beginning to sort bathroom items. He made sure to pack *Kon-Tiki* and *In My Own Way.*

Arnold followed him down the stairs. "How long

will you be gone?"

Vano's answer followed a five-second delay. "It's hard to say. Sometimes my father is unpredictable."

When they reached the lobby Arnold told him, "Mary Thorne was here earlier. She said she wanted to see you."

"Did she say what she wanted?"

"She said she had a lot of heat. What did she mean?"

Vano smiled before he answered, "I think it's mostly a matter of hormones."

"I don't know much about women," Arnold admitted, "But she sure is good looking. I hope you'll be coming back soon."

Vano's father was behind the wheel, revving the engine impatiently. Vano loaded his suitcase into the trunk. He smiled before he said to Arnold, "Don't feel bad. This may seem like a major problem but it really can't be; space and time are vast."

"You're doing it again, Vano."

"I'm not trying to do anything, though. Sometimes it feels like the words are just passing through me."

"But passing from where? From the particle people?"

At this point Vano's father began honking the horn. The honking intensified Vano's *hooommm* before he was finally able to say, "I can't be sure." He got into the car and away they went. Vano watched his dorm recede in the passenger's side mirror. From three blocks away, he could still see Arnold waving.

On the drive home, Vano's father attempted to make conversation. He said, "Don't think I'm in the dark about what's been going on. I know all about your campus misadventures."

So deep was Vano's *hooommm* there was no response which he felt he needed to make.

"I knew it was a mistake to send you off on your own to college. I warned you it was like sending out a sheep to try its luck among the wolves."

Vano said, "I'm trying to remember. I think you said it was like sending a lamb into a lion's den."

"I suppose you think that's a clever comeback."

"I'm not very good at clever comebacks. I'm trying to remember."

"Coach Radulski calls me at least twice a week. He's at the end of his rope."

The reply was, "I think the coach is very frustrated."

"Wouldn't you be? According to him, you've been sitting around like a zombie, staring into space and telling gooneybird stories about freaking aliens. Is that about it?"

Vano had to think. "I enjoy basking with Professor Meel. He's very unattached. He seems to appreciate hearing about the particle people and their perspective on the human condition. I also shared the experience with Arnold, my roommate."

"What does he think of your gibberish?"

"Arnold is very fond of the things I share with him."

"In other words, just what you don't need. Particle people from outer space. Jesus H. Christ!"

After a brief lull, Vano made the observation that "Arnold is very nice. I enjoy having him for a roommate. Robin Snook is my other roommate. He's a football star."

"It sounds like he's the one you need to be spending your time with."

"I enjoy the time I spend with Robin."

This exchange was taxing to Vernon Lucas in the extreme. He asked, "What about that chaplain? Can't he help you over some of the rough spots?"

He meant Chaplain Johansen. Vano said pleasantly, "There are no rough spots. There are only smooth spots."

"And what is that supposed to mean, not that I really want to know?"

"Rough spots are our own making," Vano explained. "According to the particle people, we don't experience enough of the spectrum. If we learned to live beyond the ego mode, we would not experience the rough spots; we would be blended with the electromagnetic spectrum."

"If you think I'm going to listen to a bunch of bullshit about blended Martians, you have another think coming."

Vano smiled the smile. He found it encouraging that the *hooommm* was firm and comfortable, even in the face of his father's considerable contempt. He decided to change the subject so he said, "I have a girlfriend. We haven't actually had a date yet, but we may have one sometime soon."

"What about Ann-Marie? Have you forgotten about her so soon? She could keep you warm on those long winter nights. I'd like to know why I didn't save myself all this grief by having you committed back in August."

There was no insight Vano could provide in connection with this speculation. Instead, he said, "Actually, I might have two girlfriends, Mary and Rita. Rita isn't as good-looking as Mary, and I'm not sure how stable she is, but I think she has a lot of money."

"*A lot of money.* You could have had enough money to buy Palm Springs. In any case, I don't intend to encourage your fantasy life."

"Mary Thorne has a very exceptional body," Vano declared.

"Never mind that, pay attention. When we have dinner, I don't want you to upset Sister Cecilia with a lot of off-the-wall blabber. She's fixing meat loaf, and she's gone to a lot of trouble."

"Meat loaf is one of my favorites," said Vano. The conversation concluded, he opened *Kon-Tiki* to chapter nine.

For dinner, Sister Cecilia served not only the meat loaf, but also mashed potatoes and gravy, garden peas with miniature onions, and frozen whipped salad. Sister asked Vano how he was enjoying college life.

"It's real nice," Vano told her.

Then she asked him about Professor Meel.

"I enjoy basking with him."

Hearing this, Vano's father stuck an index finger into each of his ears. Neither Sister nor Vano noticed. Sister asked if his college experience might be more rewarding if he worked on his homework or developed his social life or got involved in some extracurricular activities. The thrust of this inquiry was a clear indication of the coaching Vernon had given her.

Even so, Vano replied, "The ego mode prevents us from experiencing states of being. We are preoccupied with doing and achieving."

"Vano, I've never heard you talk this way before."

With his fingers still in his ears, Vano's father complained in a loud voice, "Sister, why is it that my hearing is so good? A man my age should be at least partially deaf."

Sister asked Vano, "Have you taken any of this to the Lord in prayer?"

"Any of what?"

The question caught Sister off guard; it was beyond the sphere of any coaching Vernon had provided her. "Any of anything that might be a problem," she mumbled.

Vano was lodged deep in. His standard delay preceded his answer. "Our conventional picture of God is only an ego-mode necessity. In reality, there is just the universe expanding and contracting. There are the waves, and there are the particles."

"The way you're talking, Vano. Is it really you?"

He said, "It wouldn't give me any pleasure to hurt your feelings. I hope I'm not being impolite."

"You're not being impolite, but there's no need for blasphemy."

By this time, Vano's father was pacing the room. He had a throw pillow pressed against each ear. "I'm hearing everything he says! It's a curse! If I'm 72 years old, why is my hearing so good?"

Sister Cecilia reminded him, "Actually, you're 73."

"My point exactly! If I'm losing my memory, then why can't I lose some of my hearing?"

Deciding it would be a good idea to drop the discussion entirely, Vano receded into an even deeper zone.

His father was still pacing, though. Finally, he flung away both pillows while announcing: "This is the last straw. How was he ever accepted by a college anyway? Never mind, don't answer that. I'm going to do what I should have done back in August: I'm having this kid committed."

Sister Cecilia burst into tears before she fled from the room.

*

During his first few days at *The Arbors*, Vano spent most of his time taking tests. Dr. Hicks, an ascetic-looking, hawkish man with perpetual five-o-clock shadow, administered most of Vano's tests and conducted the physiological examinations.

Vano underwent a sophisticated procedure known as *magnetic resonance imaging*, which placed him in a cocoon-like tube for almost an hour. There was no pain, but the MRI machine produced a constant racket which sounded like pneumatic hammers. When Vano was finished with the procedure, Dr. Hicks asked him if he was okay.

"I'm fine," answered Vano.

"The MRI procedure makes some people feel a little claustrophobic," said Dr. Hicks.

After his brief delay Vano said, "It was real nice. I was deep in."

"You can save your hallucinations for another time," instructed Hicks. "Eventually, you'll get your chance for all that." Then Dr. Hicks made some notes on his clipboard, opened wide, and sprayed his tongue twice with a Binaca atomizer.

The following day, Dr. Hicks asked Vano to jump up and down, hop on one foot, and touch his nose with his eyes closed. Hicks turned the lights off and looked in Vano's eyes with a tiny flashlight. He held live tuning forks next to Vano's ears just before he scraped the soles of his bare feet with a cold, sharp metal object. At the conclusion of each procedure, Hicks scrubbed his hands and forearms vigorously with antiseptic soap for 30 seconds.

When he wasn't having blood drawn, it seemed like Vano was required to take another written test. Once, when taking the MMPI, he moistened his index finger to turn the page. "Please don't do that," objected Dr. Hicks. Producing a can of Lysol disinfectant from his briefcase, he sprayed the test booklet thoroughly.

For the most part, Vano found *The Arbors* a pleasant place to be. He had no real desire to be anywhere else. In group therapy, he sat in medium *hooommm*, listening to the other patients. He spent a good deal of time sitting beneath the huge weeping willow tree on the south lawn, reading by turns from his two books. It wasn't exactly the same as basking with Oboe Meel, but it was comparable.

The day Vano was first asked to speak in group about *hooommm* was the day Herne Hill was admitted. Herne made a forceful first impression. He was a very large, thick man of 40 years, with a massive, unruly shock of hair like steel wool, and a beard to match. He wore a black leather fleece-lined vest, but no shirt. On his chest was a large tattoo of a pair of green dragons with wings and a message that read: *Live to Ride, Ride to Live.* He wore black leather trousers. His large, bronze belt buckle had these words in high relief: *Harley Fuckin Davidson.* On his feet were engineer boots festooned with straps and silver loops.

Herne Hill also carried a shiny brass French horn, clamped firmly under his right arm.

Mrs. Applewhite asked, "Do you mean to say that this man is going to be a member of our group?"

Dr. Burgemeister looked Hill over from top to bottom. "How did you get this way?" he asked.

Hill did not find this to be an impertinent question. He explained by saying, "When I was growing up down in Long Beach, my daddy was a biker in a gang that went around terrorizing small towns in the desert. Then when I was still a prepubescent, he got a new old lady, this flower chick who was into granny dresses and throwing red paint onto women wearing fur coats."

He paused long enough to take a Twinkie package from his pants pocket. He concluded by saying, "I had to grow up under the influence of this parental dichotomy." Unwrapping the package, he shoved one of the Twinkies whole into his mouth.

One of the patients, Baker, told Herne Hill that he

too had grown up in Orange County. This information pleased Herne. He and Baker exchanged a bro handshake and a high five. Dr. Hicks asked, "What's the French horn for?"

"I'll show you," said Hill. He put the instrument to his mouth and began playing in round tones the famous part of the *Blue Danube Waltz.*

When he was finished with the piece, Mrs. Applewhite said, "Oh my! Is he going to be in our group for very long?"

In response to her question, Herne played one more selection, the famous part of the *Dance of the Sugar Plum Fairies.* Upon its conclusion, Dr. Hicks said, "That's very nice, Mr. Hill, but what is it *for?*"

"Didn't I just show you? I like to play the horn, Man."

Dr. Burgemeister interrupted to suggest, "Why don't you sit down, Mr. Hill?" Dr. Burgemeister was a grandfatherly man with tufts of white hair forming bushy crescents above his ears. The other two staff members, Dr. Hicks and Nurse Cubbage, were seated on either side of him. Nurse Cubbage was a stout woman of middle age who wore a no-nonsense look.

Burgemeister explained, "Mr. Hill, the young man seated next to you is Vano. When you arrived, he was beginning to tell us about hoom. Please feel free to contribute in any way you can."

"What is hoom?" inquired Herne Hill.

But before there was opportunity to answer, a patient named Gayle stood straight up out of her chair and complained in a loud voice, "I'm not sitting next to him! He's playing with himself again!"

"Calm down," said Dr. Hicks.

"John is playing pocket pool again and I'm not

sitting next to him!"

"Do you suppose anyone else wants to sit by him?"

"I said pocket pool! Don't you get it, it's *pocket pool*! I ain't sitting next to him!"

Herne Hill spoke up: "Here's an empty chair next to mine. Bring the little bugger on over."

"Are you sure?"

"Hell, yes. I enjoy a little ball and chain as much as the next guy."

"Thank you for helping with the seating problem," said Dr. Hicks to Hill. "But we can do nicely without the sophomoric humor."

Hill didn't speak, but raised the French horn to his mouth. He blew a *fortissimo* F sharp.

"We can do without that, as well." said Hicks.

Gayle took John by the arm. She pulled him to his feet, led him to the empty seat beside Herne Hill, and sat him down. John was utterly compliant. Tall and thin, with a chop job of unruly brown hair, he was deaf and without speech. His right eye, a wholesale cataract, looked like a cloudy globe of eggwhite; no pupil or iris was discernible. His left eye was a partial cataract. The staff assumed he had some light and shade vision in it. John sat down beside Herne Hill, resumed his pocket pool, and said, "Lllllll."

"Now then," said Dr. Hicks. "If everyone is quite comfortable, maybe we can get something accomplished."

Dr. Burgemeister accepted the cue. He turned to Vano Lucas once again and said, "Vano, we'd like to hear about hoom."

On Vano's face was the pleasant, bland smile. It was some moments before he readied his reply: "It's not hoom, it's *hooommm*."

"Whatever," said Dr. Hicks, annoyed. "Why does it take you so long to answer questions?"

After five seconds Vano said, "I'm in *hooommm*. When I'm in deep it takes time for questions and answers to get processed. There's nothing wrong with the answers, but it takes time."

"We'd like to know what hoom is," said Dr. Burgemeister.

"*Hooommm*." Vano corrected him.

"Whatever," said Hicks again. "Do you intend to tell us, or shall we just play 20 questions?"

Vano maintained the smile. After five seconds he said, "*Hooommm* is a state of mind. It's a mental zone. It can be a transcendent zone. It is something like hypnosis or going numb; it is something like a trance. It is like all those things, but also different from each one of them. *Hooommm* is a mental zone unlike any other experience."

"But what does it mean?" insisted Hicks. "And can you please speed up with the answers?"

It took a while, but then, "I'm not sure if it has a meaning. Looking for meaning may be the flaw. It's more a state of being. Sometimes in *hooommm*, the sky gets orange. Sometimes there is vibration and resonance like a baritone singing voice in a shower stall made of fiberglass. It's because of the resonance I named it *hooommm*."

"Did you say the sky gets orange?" Dr. Burgemeister inquired.

"Not the whole sky, usually just the rim of the sky. It's like a bright orange sunset on the horizon, only all the horizons are orange at the same time, in all directions. Sometimes the sky gets a heavy texture, like it's made of lava."

"I see," said Burgemeister. "Can you remember the first time you went into, uh, the first time it happened to you?"

Vano said, "I can remember vividly the first time I

went into deep *hooommm*. If you want, I could tell you about it."

"Deep hoom?"

Vano could see no further need to correct pronunciation. "The first time I ever went in deep was only a few weeks ago. Before that, I was just in shallow. There were times last spring when I had brief periods of vibration, but they were only like forerunners of *hooommm*. They never developed into an actual zone."

Dr. Burgemeister removed his glasses slowly. He began cleaning them with lens cleaner. "Maybe we'd better start at the beginning. Why don't you tell us something about the forerunners?"

Dr. Hicks buried his face in his hands. Baker, who had fallen asleep, began to snore in his chair. John said, "Llllll."

Vano began, "There was the time about the end of May. We were on our senior class trip at Magic Mountain. I was standing under the sky chute when a girl fell out of her harness. She fell all the way down and landed on the blacktop real close to me. She was wearing a white blouse and blue shorts. Her whole body just busted apart. There was blood and guts on the pavement like a run-over possum on the road."

"Jesus Christ!" exclaimed Herne Hill. "Big time roadkill! That's a great fucking story."

"And then what?" asked Burgemeister.

"I just looked all around me. Everybody was going about their business. All the rides were still going, people were buying hot dogs and Polish sausages, all that amusement park stuff. There was this group of strolling banjo players playing songs, and some actors in gorilla costumes were goofing on little kids and giving them candy. That's when I went into a very shallow *hooommm*. I could see and hear everything, but it was like everything was housed in this chamber of vibrations. Everything seemed unreal, and there was no emotion connected to anything."

"And then what?"

"That's about it. I just stood there in *hooommm*, looking all around, and everything seemed to be whizzing. It only lasted a few minutes, then I was myself again."

"That's a great fucking story," said Herne Hill. Hill whacked John on the thigh before he said, "Isn't that a killer story, Little Buddy?" Turning toward Dr. Hicks, he said, "I figure me 'n' John is going to be *compadres* in no time flat."

"How fortuitous," replied Hicks, without lifting his face from his hands.

"That's very interesting," Burgemeister told Vano. "Now maybe you could tell us about the time when you had the deep one."

Vano was still smiling. "I'd be happy to," he said. He took the time to gather himself first. "It happened with our housekeeper, Sister Cecilia. She's about thirty something. She has a last name, but I'm not sure what it is. Ever since she started playing in the Salvation Army band, she just goes by Sister."

Dr. Hicks interrupted by holding up his wristwatch. "We really don't have all day, Vano. Is there any way you could speed this up?"

"She's really a Catholic, though; it seems like a paradox, doesn't it?"

"The rest of it, please?"

Vano told the whole story, precisely as it had happened, the night before he left for college. He tried to quote Sister word-for-word, although he couldn't rely absolutely on the accuracy of his memory. He concluded by saying, "When I left her room, I went to my own room and entered the deepest *hooommm* I'd ever known. The earth seemed to vibrate and there was a throbbing orange glow. After I went to sleep I had the dream about the pyramid. Of course all this happened after the accident with Jose's bat."

Herne Hill whacked himself on both thighs and exclaimed,"*Hot damn*! That's *another* great story!"

Briefly, Burgemeister was tempted to try and untangle the bats and pyramid threads, but decided he'd be wiser to stay the course by doing first things first. He asked Vano, "How long were you in this deep hoom?"

Again, Vano didn't bother to correct the pronunciation. "I was in for good after that. I've never been out."

"And what do you do in hoom?"

"I do the same things I usually do. I go to classes, do my homework, read my books, talk to friends. Even if I'm in deep, I do all the things I usually do. It's just the state of mind that's different."

"Jesus fucking Christ," said Herne Hill. "That's one of the best stories I ever heard. Is it true?"

"Mr. Hill, this is not the hot stove league," said Dr. Hicks acidly. "We don't put people in group therapy so they can invent stories. This is not the neighborhood poker game."

Hill raised his French horn long enough to blow a sour note in Dr. Hicks' direction.

Dr. Burgemeister asked, "Does anybody have anything to say to Vano? Are there any questions?"

"Yeah, you bet." said Herne. "I'd like to hear a little more about Sister Cecilia's tits."

"Oh my!" exclaimed Mrs. Applewhite.

Nurse Cubbage spoke up for the first time. "This is preposterous," she declared.

Vano turned in Dr. Burgemeister's direction. "Do you want me to go into more detail about Sister's tits?"

"I don't think that will be necessary."

"How 'bout her bush, then?" Hill persisted. "He never said word one about her bush."

"This man is exceedingly vulgar!" proclaimed Mrs. Applewhite. "Do you mean to say that he's going to be in our group every single day?"

Perceiving that Mrs. Applewhite did not approve of him, Herne Hill turned the bell of his instrument near her ear and blew a piercing A flat. Mrs. Applewhite bolted from her chair like a missile and collided with Nurse Cubbage. The impact, which sent both women to the floor, also scattered the nurse's papers and folders. From the prone position she protested, "This is preposterous!"

Dr. Burgemeister decided it was time to end the session. "We are dismissed for today!" he announced in a loud voice.

The session concluded, the staff returned to a conference room for the post-mortem. Burgemeister sat on one side of the table, Hicks on the other. Nurse Cubbage occupied the end of the table nearest the window.

At the other end of the table sat Herne Hill.

Burgemeister assumed a grave countenance. He chewed the tip of his Bic pen thoughtfully before he said, "The Vano Lucas case is intriguing, to say the least. The delusional pattern is provocative. We seem to be dealing with disorganized cognitive process as well as some withdrawal. It may be a form of undifferentiated schizophrenia on the subacute level. It may even have a catatonic element."

Dr. Hicks sighed aloud. He wondered for the umpteenth time why he had chosen to spend his life farting around with society's lunatics. But then he remembered: *I do it for the money.* This recovery established, he said, "Let's increase his medication."

Nurse Cubbage, who was studying Vano's chart, said, "He's not on any medication."

Dr. Hicks produced a vial of nose drops. He began irrigating his right nostril. "So there's the problem then. What's the point of having a patient and no medication?"

Still pensive, Dr. Burgemeister continued, "It must be some form of schizophreniform disorder, undifferentiated type. There's a catatonic element involved, or I'll put in with you!"

The three staff members were suddenly startled by the loud voice of Herne Hill, from the end of the table: "Maybe he's just a numbnuts."

Turning abruptly, they noticed Hill for the first time. "What the hell do you think you're doing here??" demanded Dr. Hicks.

"Just trying to be helpful, I suppose."

Hicks said caustically, "For your information, the term *numbnuts* is not included in the *Diagnostic and Statistical Manual*. Furthermore, you have no business in this room."

Without a word, Hill handed Dr. Hicks a white card the size of a calling card, whereupon Hicks read its printed message:

You are a suck-off

After pocketing the card, Hicks ordered Herne Hill to leave the room, which he did promptly.

Hicks stood up to close the door after him. Turning back to his two colleagues, he asked, "Do we have any recommendations for Vano Lucas?"

Hicks flushed his left nostril while waiting for an answer, but none was forthcoming. He capped the bottle. "I've got a 2:30 tee time. Let's increase his medication and keep an eye on him."

*

It wasn't until four days later in group that Dr. Burgemeister got around to asking Vano for more information about *hooommm*. Burgemeister, Dr. Hicks, and Nurse Cubbage arrived in the day room where patients were watching *Sylvester and Tweetie* cartoons. Dr. Hicks switched off the set. "Let's get started, shall we?"

Burgemeister suggested that it might be helpful if the group could know a little more about Vano's lifestyle. He asked Vano how he liked to spend his time.

"I spend most of my time deep in," explained Vano. "I like to read and I like to contemplate."

"You say reading and contemplation. What do you like to read?"

Following his customary pause, Vano said, "I like to read about religions, philosophy, and the supernatural. I'm currently reading *Kon-Tiki* and *In My Own Way*. As for contemplation, I like to contemplate the things I read about. When I'm basking with Oboe Meel, sometimes I just like to absorb the conversation which surrounds me." Vano smiled the pleasant smile.

Burgemeister said, "I take it hoom is not unpleasant."

"*Hooommm* is very pleasant," answered Vano. "Especially deep in. It has a certain transcendence to it."

Dr. Hicks was losing what little patience he had. "It may seem pleasant, but it happens to be a very serious problem. Do you understand that?"

Vano smiled. "It must seem to be," he said.

"It's turning you into a zero, a cipher, a non-entity, a vegetable. It's making you invisible. Do you understand what I'm telling you?"

It took a while before he could construct an answer. He finally said, "In my brain I can understand the point you are making, but it lacks emotional impact because I'm hearing you from deep in. I wouldn't want to offend you, but you are a tiny blip on the distant side of a vast landscape. Your words are as neutral as grains of sand."

Hicks stood up abruptly and began to pace. "Where is Hill?" he asked. "Where is Herne Hill?"

"He's down in the print shop," Gayle informed him.

Hicks made the observation that Herne spent too much time in the print room. "He is a member of this group, the same as anyone else."

"Can't we just leave him down there?" suggested Mrs. Applewhite.

Hicks ignored this option when he said to Vano, "Would you please go get him?"

"I'd be happy to get him," was Vano's pleasant reply. He left the room to fetch Herne Hill.

No sooner did Vano leave the room than Baker arrived. He was carrying a split-leaf philidendron, four feet tall, in a large clay pot.

"What is that?" Hicks asked him.

Instead of answering, Baker walked swiftly so as to occupy the seat next to Gayle.

"You can't bring that in here," Hicks continued; "There's no telling what debris it might be carrying."

"Besides that, you're late." added Dr. Burgemeister. "This group begins promptly at nine o'clock."

Baker peered at the staffers from between the generous leaves. "I'm only late by 15 minutes. Dr. Radabiancakrishna says it would be good for me to be less compulsive."

Hicks produced a small bottle of Murine and began applying eyedrops. "You can't bring that in here. The invisible flotsam and jetsam must be enormous."

"It would be a good idea for you to be less compulsive, I agree with that," said Dr. Burgemeister. "But if we want to have a successful group, we need to begin promptly."

"Who is Dr. Radabiancakrishna?" asked Nurse Cubbage.

"He's a new consult," said Hicks. "Get that thing out of here," he directed Baker.

"I ain't sitting next to a plant," said Gayle firmly.

Hicks was out of patience again. "A few days ago, you refused to sit next to John. Maybe you'd like to draw up a seating chart."

Baker said, "Dr. Radabiancakrishna says it's okay for me to have a placebo. It gives me confidence."

"That is a plant, not a placebo. I'm only going to say this one more time: take it out of here." Hicks screwed the cap back in place on his eyedrop bottle before returning it to the inside pocket of his jacket. Baker left in a huff, without speaking.

Vano returned with Herne Hill. Hill was still wearing his leather ensemble, but in addition, he wore a printer's apron. He took an aggressive look around the room, then turned on the television and exclaimed: "Hot damn! Sylvester and Tweetie!"

Dr. Hicks immediately turned it off. "If you don't mind, we are trying to conduct group."

Herne Hill did mind. "Watch this," he said to Dr. Hicks. He picked up a square, green ashtray and sailed it like a frisbee through a window. The sound of shattering glass was frightening.

"Lllllll." said John.

"Okay," said Dr. Burgemeister. "For that outburst, you lose your television privileges for the whole weekend. What do you think of that?"

Herne Hill folded his arms across his chest; he was staring at his engineer boots. "You can't take away my TV privileges," he declared. "I have unlimited TV privileges. As a matter of fact, I have *lifetime* TV privileges."

"Oh, is that so?"

"Yes it's so."

"And who authorized these TV privileges, I'd like to know?"

"Nurse Cubbage did," asserted Herne Hill. "I gave her a dry hump in the kitchen. She wanted to return the favor, so she gave me special TV privileges."

"This is preposterous!" snorted Nurse Cubbage.

"What's a dry hump?" asked Burgemeister.

"This is preposterous!" repeated the nurse.

"That's where you hump 'em, but with all your clothes still on," explained Hill. "If you actually shoot your wad, it gets kind of messy."

"This is preposterous!"

"It's not only that, it's also vulgar," Mrs. Applewhite pointed out.

Dr. Hicks could stand no more. "*Do* you all mind terribly?? Maybe we could return to the business of this group?"

Even though intrigued by the phenomenon known as dry humping, Burgemeister recognized the wisdom of Dr. Hicks' suggestion. He said, "Let's do just that." He turned again to Vano Lucas.

"Vano, there's an important piece of your hoom experience which you haven't shared with the group. Would you like to tell us about the particular people?"

"It was the particle people," said Vano, "Not the particular people."

"Fine. Tell us about the particle people."

"I only had one visit with the particle people. I was on my way out of the coma. I only had one conversation with them. You might say they live in space, or you might say space lives in them. They can break themselves down into their individual atomic particles. They move throughout the universe at the speed of light."

"I see," said Burgemeister, wondering if in truth he saw anything at all.

Vano continued, after a short hiatus: "Sometimes the diffused particles can come together. When such a coalition occurs, the particle people can assume a humanoid shape."

Dr. Hicks sighed audibly just before he buried his face in his hands. He said to himself, *Oh my god.*

At this point, Herne Hill rose from his chair. He fished out a small white card, about the size of a business card, from his apron pocket, and presented it to Dr. Burgemeister without speaking. Dr. Burgemeister read the printing on the card:

Pisces: hold your water and keep a tight asshole.

Herne returned quietly to his seat. Dr. Burgemeister made no comment about the card, but slid it into his jacket pocket.

Gayle was curious. Her question for Vano was, "What do the particle people look like?"

"They look like a collection of tiny lights. Tiny as pinpoints. When they coalesce, the lights twinkle more rapidly."

"What conversation did you have with the particle people?" asked Burgemeister.

"After they explained to me about the particle mode, they informed me that human beings living on earth live in the ego mode. It's because of the ego mode handicap that human relationships usually don't work out. They said that the logical side of *hooommm* was the understanding of the ego mode and the particle mode."

"They knew about hoom?"

"In a sense, *hooommm* is what they *are*. It was because of my experience in *hooommm* that they contacted me. They even told me of something they call *ultimate hooommm.*"

"What is ultimate hoom?"

"I don't know. The particle people told me that they were only giving me a partial understanding of the true meaning of existence. They told me they hoped that some day my understanding would be complete."

Dr. Hicks' face was still buried. Without looking up he said, "I've seen some disorganized cognitive process in my time, but this takes the cake. And I do mean *fruitcake*, if you get my drift."

Herne Hill rose once again to bring Dr. Burgemeister another card. His mission accomplished, he returned quietly to his seat. Burgemeister read the card:

If you hope for longevity, drink the water with the extra molecule; find the heavy water.

The printing was very neat and regular, as had been the case with the earlier card. Burgemeister put it into his pocket before he turned back to Vano. "You say the particle people talked to you about fundamental truths. Does this mean you believe you spoke to God?"

Vano had no idea this question was meant to locate him within the classic paradigm of delusional disorganization. He smiled before he answered, "They say on planets like ours, people imagine a big man in the sky. But in truth, there is just the universe, expanding and contracting. There are the waves, and there are the particles. They told me the Book of Revelation is just a small fragment of a long epic poem from an advanced people who inhabited the earth millions of years ago."

"God damn," said Herne Hill. "Does this guy tell great fucking stories or what?" With this remark, Hill rose a third time to bring Dr. Burgemeister another printed card. Burgemeister read it to himself:

Show me the crevices in your hands and feet. Consider the cats which scavenge the dumpsters in your neighborhood.

Dr. Hicks had reached the end of his rope. He went and stood in front of Herne Hill. Palm up, he held out his hand. "Give me the cards. All of them."

Sullenly, Herne handed Hicks four printed cards.

"Watch this," said Hicks. Savagely, he tore all four cards into the tiniest bits he could manage, then threw them into an ashtray. "Now, maybe, we can get something accomplished."

But nothing further was accomplished. When the session was over, the staff went back to a conference room, while Vano followed Herne Hill down to the first floor. Like a shadow, John trailed behind, making his sightless way down the stairs by hanging onto Herne's apron strings.

Hill took out a plastic MCI card and began to ply it in the locked door of the print room. "I think we need to have a talk, *mi amigo*," he said to Vano.

Vano didn't answer. In medium *hooommm*, he read the large red sign on the print room door:

ABSOLUTELY NO ADMITTANCE

Herne was deft with the credit card. The door swung open. As soon as he turned on the lights he said, "I'm going to need the resources of this print room while I'm here." He began opening cabinets.

Vano suggested, "Maybe it's not wise to be here without permission. If you get caught there could be serious consequences."

"More serious than being locked up in the puzzle house? Here--have a card." He gave Vano one of the heavy water cards. "If it makes you feel any better, we'll put John here at the door. He'll be our lookout." Saying this, Herne led John into position at the threshold.

Eventually, when words came, Vano said, "But John is blind. Do you think he'll make an effective lookout?"

"He may be a little shaky at his post, but he'll have fun. I've cut the pockets out of his pants so he can have direct access. He's going to be into some ball and chain, big time."

"I see."

Hill gave it a wave of the hand. "Have no fear, *amigo*. I doubt if the staff here can find their ass with both hands. Anyway, we need to talk about your thing. Your hoom."

Vano followed Herne to the paper cutter. If people insisted on saying it wrong, it was okay with him. "I've tried to explain *hooommm* in our group. I can't think of much more to say about it, but I'm willing to try, if you'd like."

Herne Hill said, "I've heard enough to tell you this: I think you've been contacted by the Federation."

Vano's vibrations intensified as if a switch had been

thrown in his brain. He finally asked, "The Federation?"

"That's what I'm sayin'. Either they've contacted you or you've contacted them. However you put it, it's the same result." Hill was stacking expensive stacks of bond flannel paper next to the cutter. It took Vano several moments to find his tongue:

"But I don't know what the Federation is."

"It's a group consciousness thing. It's made up of these thousands of beings who are on a very high plane. They're highly evolved. They don't need words to communicate. Some people are lucky enough to enter their flow of vibrations. I think you might be one of them--that's what your hoom is telling you. Here, have a look at this." Herne was showing Vano a sketch of a small building flanked by standards with large circles. It looked like a futuristic fast-food restaurant, but Vano was located in so deep that it took several moments to absorb any of the building's particulars.

"This is the prototype of the *Arcane Express*," Hill explained.

Vano wasn't ready to shift gears. He asked him, "Who are the beings that make up the Federation?"

"Some of them are flesh and blood people, walking around on earth. But most of them are spirit beings who live in another dimension. If you get into their flow, you can feed on their vibrations."

Vano felt swallowed up by the rich, orange vibes. "Do you think this is the meaning of *hooommm*, then?"

"I thought so from the first time I heard you speak of it, *Amigo*. In fact, it may be that you're already a Federation member. I've heard tell that some people are in it for quite a while before they even realize it."

Vano remained silent while Hill showed him some more drawings. "The *Arcane Express* is going to be a franchise business which I intend to start as soon as I get out of here."

"You mean like McDonald's?"

"In a way, but we'll be doing readings and charts instead of burgers and fries. You see the circles here on top of these standards? Each one of these is going to be a marquee *yin and yang*."

"It looks real nice," said Vano. "Does the Federation have a purpose?"

"Since the Federation is on a higher plane, I think they work to uplift the human condition." Then Hill began speaking of business cards and letterheads, but Vano was removed to a zone so remote he heard very few of the details.

*

It was shortly after lunch when Vano's father arrived at the *Arbors* to meet in conference with the three staff members. The meeting opened with the congenial accoutrements of tea and cookies, but it didn't take long for Vernon to get pissed.

"I can't tell you how grateful I am for all you've done for Vano," said Mr. Lucas. "I'm so grateful that he's well now."

Dr. Burgemeister registered a nervous smile before saying, "Well, we aren't saying that he's well *per se*, but we think he might do better at home."

"If you're sending him home, he must be well."

"Well, not precisely." Burgemeister swallowed before continuing, "We believe Vano has suffered from some kind of trauma which has manifested itself in certain elements of schizophrenia and certain elements of catatonia. Much of it seems to be on the subacute level."

"What is that gobblydegook supposed to mean?" demanded Vernon.

Dr. Hicks explained, "What Dr. Burgemeister is getting at is that we have no idea what's the matter with your son."

"No idea you say?"

"Not the foggiest."

Mr. Lucas stiffened his back. "I think you should know," he said, "That I'm a very busy man. Strictly speaking, I'm retired from my corporation, but I have a large investment portfolio to manage. Furthermore, I do consulting work with CEOs in various parts of the country, which puts me on the frequent flyer roster. In short, I don't have a lot of time to waste on Vano's mental health. How do you evaluate his blow to the head?"

All three staff members exchanged blank stares. "Blow to the head?" asked Burgemeister thoughtfully.

"He got hit in the head by Jose Canseco's bat!!" shrieked Vernon Lucas. "What in hell do you think this is all about!?"

Burgemeister chewed his pen. While he was trying to formulate an answer, Vernon escalated: "Vano was the greatest pitcher alive! He might still be again! He was hit in the head by a baseball bat, which knocked him into a coma! What do you think this is all about?"

The long, embarrassing silence which ensued was finally broken by Nurse Cubbage who said, "He never wants to talk about the past."

"That's right," said Dr. Hicks. "According to your son, there is no such thing as the past. There is only the present moment."

Burgemeister extended the pensive mode which

claimed him by ruminating aloud: "Actually, that's not quite it either. The present is only the transforming instant when future becomes past."

Vernon was flabbergasted. "What are you, a bunch of idiots?! What am I paying you for? Jesus Christ!" But he was out of breath; he fumbled for his pills.

Noting the scarlet condition of Vernon's scalp, Nurse Cubbage expressed concern for his health: "Are you on medication, Sir?"

"Yes, yes, I'm a heart patient. Never mind that. Does he want to go home? Is that what you're saying?"

"I asked him that this morning," replied Hicks. "I asked him if he didn't think it was time to return to the real world."

"What did he say?"

"He said, 'places are places.'"

Vernon groaned as he covered his face. "Places are places," he whimpered.

"Would you care for a glass of water?" the nurse asked him.

Vernon ignored her. He said to the group, "So tell me: if you have no idea what's the matter with him, then what's to be done with him?"

Burgemeister took over again. "We've tried a number of therapeutic techniques, and we have tried Vano on medication. None of these efforts has produced quite the result we might have hoped for."

"Of course," sighed Lucas Senior.

"There is much important research being done in San Francisco and other places in the area of brain chemistry and synapse dysfunction. There are several neurological tests which might be worth a try."

Hicks broke in to say, "What Dr. Burgemeister is trying to say is that we have no idea what should be done for your son."

Mr. Lucas' back stiffened again before he said, "Let me tell you a little history. When Vano came along, it was just one of those accidents people have to put up with. My wife was in the hospital for appendicitis. When she came home, she had an infant with her. That infant was Vano. She found him in the hospital lost and found. She felt sorry for him, so she brought him home."

"Oh my," said Nurse Cubbage. "You mean he was just in with a bunch of scarves and gloves and car keys?"

"That's about the size of it. Nobody ever did claim him. I was 55 years old at the time; I was not inclined to be a parent and god knows not interested in learning how. I said to my wife at the time, I said, 'You found him, you can raise him.' She said that was fine with her, she took care of all parenting, but then she died when the boy was only eight. We've had housekeepers ever since that time, and whatever parenting needed to be done, it was their job to take care of it. I've tried to throw enough resources Vano's way to give him a comfortable lifestyle. Am I getting through to you people?"

"Certainly, Sir." Nurse Cubbage assured him.

"Even more than you realize," added Dr. Hicks.

Vernon rubbed his eyes before he continued. He looked as if he might begin crying at any moment. "He was the greatest pitcher alive. He might still be again. The time he's spent in here will cost me a small fortune, but you people are telling me you have no recommendation what to do with him."

"I can give you a recommendation," said Dr. Hicks.

"Okay, let's hear it. What do I do?"

"Do nothing," answered Hicks.

"Do nothing?"

"Do anything. Do with him what you would have

done if he'd never come here."

"Well, what the hell. It would be cheaper to send him back to Entrada than it would be to keep him here. He's not going to spend his time hanging around the house, I'll goddam guarantee you that."

Dr. Burgemeister approved with a broad smile. "That sounds fine. Send him back to college, just as if none of this had ever happened. The real world may be just what he needs."

"You should've been there," said Lucas Senior. "Vano blew away every Oakland hitter like it was little league. The 20 million signing bonus was right there on Rakestraw's clipboard, where everyone could see."

All three staff members had to wonder by this time whether Vernon's fantasies weren't perhaps even more enchanted than his son's. The one thing Hicks knew for sure, though, was that there was an opening to conclude the meeting: "Vano is on a field trip with the other members of his unit," he said to Lucas Senior. "You could pick him up tomorrow at about this time."

Chapter Six

All 32 patients on Vano's unit participated in the field trip to the zoo. Nurse Cubbage was the staff person in charge. After spending a brief period of time looking at the grizzly bears, the group made its way to the primate house.

In the primate house, they happened upon Professor Revuelto, who was convening his cultural anthropology class in front of two chimpanzee cages. Robin Snook, Mary Thorne, and Arnold Beeker were among the students Vano recognized immediately.

"I know these people," said Vano to Herne Hill. "Two of them are my roommates at Entrada. This is my anthropology class."

"Hot damn," said Hill. "Life's a beach, ain't it?"

Professor Revuelto was mounting a rostrum to gain some height. He wore a maroon beret at a rakish angle, and a paisley neck scarf. He didn't recognize the group of mental patients standing in such close proximity, but he did enjoy any contingency which might increase the size of his audience. He raised his arms for silence, then began to speak:

"Today we examine the phenomenon of the flexible thumb, and its crucial contribution to the development of our species. What more appropriate backdrop could there be than that provided by these great apes, who stand here as vivid reminders of our long evolutionary process?"

Revuelto paused long enough to wiggle his thumb at the members of the class. "A flexible thumb is something we take for granted," he noted. "We never give it a second

thought."
    Before he could continue, Revuelto was approached by a zoo man. The man asked, "What do you think you're doing?"
    Revuelto replied, "I am a professor from Entrada College. These are anthropology students. We are here to study evolutionary process."
    The name *Hank* was scripted in yellow thread above the zoo man's left shirt pocket; he wore a navy blue cap that looked like a policeman's cap. "I'm not sure you can do this," he said. "I'll have to talk to my superiors."
    "*Madre de Dios!*" exclaimed Revuelto. "I conduct this lecture here every year! I've been doing so for 20 years."
    "Like I say," Hank repeated, "I'll have to talk to my superiors. I'll be right back."
    During this exchange, Robin Snook moved closer to Vano, clapped him on the back, and asked him when he was getting out of the looney bin.
    "Sometime soon," Vano said. "I'm not exactly sure when, though."
    This information pleased Robin, so he gave Vano another whack between the shoulder blades. Vano introduced Robin to Herne Hill. "It's nice that the two of you can meet one another," he said. "It may be that you have a lot in common."
    Robin and Herne exchanged a high five.
    Using a loud voice, Revuelto reasserted his control of the class. "Pay no attention to the interruption," he advised the students, "impertinent though it may be. The development of the flexible thumb was a crucial event in human evolution. Walking upright, with a flexible thumb, *homo sapiens* found a greatly increased capacity for gripping and balance. This quite naturally led to an increased capacity

for hunting, making tools, using tools, and making weapons. Neither the phenomenon of man as hunter nor man as farmer could have occurred without the development of a flexible thumb."

Robin Snook said to Vano, "What he's saying here might be important."

Vano was very deep in, but he managed to reply, "It might be very important."

Revuelto continued, "Most of what we call human progress could not have happened without the flexible thumb. The things we think of as simple, such as washing dishes, baking bread, building a house, whittling a stick, even our sports and games. We could never have had these activities."

"Now I *know* this is important," insisted Robin Snook.

Hank the zoo worker returned to inform Professor Revuelto, "I couldn't find my immediate superior. I'm going to have to take this straight to the top; it could take some time."

Robin asked Revuelto if there could be football without the flexible thumb.

"Of course not," answered the professor. "None of our modern games which require gripping, or throwing, or catching, would be possible without the flexible thumb development."

"I was just thinking," said Robin, "But couldn't you play the line without a flexible thumb? Of course no way could you play the backfield without one, but you might be able to play the line."

Revuelto smiled indulgently in Robin's direction before saying, "Mr. Snook, you are missing the point. Our modern sports and games would not even *exist* without the flexible thumb development."

"Don't get me wrong, I don't mean the defensive line, I'm just sayin' the offensive line. See, in the offensive line you can't use your hands anyway. When you block, you have to keep your hands in here, like this."

"Mr. Snook, trust me on this."

"Of course you couldn't play center, I'll grant you that. The center has to snap the ball and no way to do that without a thumb. What it boils down to is you could play offensive guard or tackle without a flexible thumb."

Revuelto's patience was wearing thin. "That ought to be more than enough discussion of football, I feel quite sure."

Herne Hill spoke up: "I'm with you, Bro. What I'd like to know is, could you whack off with no flexible thumb?"

"*Madre de Dios!*" bellowed the professor. "I order you people to clear out immediately! This is an anthropology class."

The chimpanzee behind Revuelto and to his right had achieved a semi-erection; he began to wave his pecker. John, Herne Hill's *little buddy*, was standing next to Nurse Cubbage. He unzipped his pants and began to wave his own pecker.

John had a substantial organ. When the nurse helped him return it to his pants, she extended the procedure longer than necessary. She declared to no one in particular, "We've always assumed that John was completely blind. If he's mimicking the chimp, it could mean that he has some partial vision. We'll have to review the possibility at the next staffing."

John said, "Lllllll."

Recognizing the urgent need to recover control, Revuelto repeated his clearing-out order. He might have been successful in this attempt, but the larger of the two chimps got a firm grip on his scarf, gave a forceful yank, and twirled the professor in the direction of the cage. Pinned against the iron bars and crimson faced, Revuelto began to squeal for help.

"I think this lecture is over," said Robin to Vano. "Why don't you just come back with us?"

Vano was deep in. The long delay came before his answer, "I haven't been released from *The Arbors* yet."

Robin pressed him. "What difference could a few days make? You might as well come with us."

Vano tried to think of a reason not to comply with the suggestion. "I might as well come with you," he repeated numbly. He said goodbye to Herne and rode back to Entrada in one of the vans.

*

During his first two days back on campus, Vano went to classes and spent a little time browsing in the campus book store. Most of his time, though, was spent on the quad in deepest *hooommm.* For reasons unclear, the primate house experience had precipitated a fiery orange event which was nearly tactile. Molten layers of lava were tiered along the sky, encircling the campus. A deep rumbling seemed to quiver the firmament.

Occasionally, he was joined by Oboe Meel, but very little conversation passed between them. Once Oboe spoke of his new office and another time he said something about philosophy tests, but Vano was in far too deep to respond. He thought of Dr. Hicks' words: "This is turning you into a non-entity." But maybe it was a different entity.

On the third day, Vano returned to the dorm room

where he sat at Arnold Beeker's desk. He entered some data on Arnold's computer and watched the words as they formed on the monitor screen:

> *The Jane Fonda Workout Book*
> *Thin Thighs in Thirty Days*
> *Looking Out for Number One*
> *The Late, Great Planet Earth*
> *If You aren't Worth it, Who Is?*
> *The Girl Who Fell from her Harness*
> *How to Pick up Girls*
> *The Clouds Go Right On*
> *The Wendy Dilemma*

In deep, Vano stared at the screen. He stared at the monitor against a backdrop of bubbling orange flares. The room began to vibrate, but it wasn't scary; he sat in utter passivity.

Then suddenly, the monitor cleared itself, one line at a time, until the screen was blank. It remained blank for 30 seconds. Then, in place of Vano's entries, a new one appeared, squarely in the center of the screen:

Evolution

Vano stared on, thinking of Revuelto's flexible thumb lecture. He deleted the word *evolution*, then made another entry of his own, once again taking care to center it:

The Flexible Thumb

Still locked down ever so deep on deep, Vano was prepared to wait with ultra patience. After 30 seconds, the monitor cleared again and the *evolution* entry made another appearance. Vano couldn't help thinking to himself, *we are blended with the entire electromagnetic spectrum. We are the waves and we are the particles.* Way on down inside, deepest and sublime, Vano stared at the screen for two hours.

Then Arnold Beeker entered the room. "I've just been over at the union," he announced. "The spelunking club is organizing its first outing."

Vano didn't reply. He continued staring at the screen.

Arnold was wearing a white dress shirt with the sleeves rolled up. He lay back on his bed and began cleaning chin pimples with a Stridex medicated pad. "I've been doing some thinking," he disclosed. "I think gravity may be the key to the whole thing."

It took several seconds before Vano was able to turn his attention in Arnold's direction. "You're still fascinated with *ultimate hooommm,* aren't you?"

"Who wouldn't be? Professor Revuelto wrote a manuscript last year about folds in the earth. It hasn't been published yet, so if anyone wanted to read it, they'd have to borrow it from him."

"How do you know about Professor Revuelto's manuscript?" asked Vano.

"It's the kind of thing I know about, Vano. See, Revuelto has this theory that there are folds in the earth that can possibly lead to different planes of existence. If you pass through one of the folds, you might wake up three days later on the other side of the globe, or even on another planet. But you wouldn't know how you got there."

Vano smiled. "When the book is published, I would enjoy reading it."

"*If* it gets published might be more like it." Arnold was fidgeting with the blue and gold Rubik's cube which served him as a paperweight. He said, "I'm afraid Revuelto is on the wrong track, to tell you the truth. What he calls folds in the earth may only be weak spots in the earth's gravitational field. The fissures are extremely narrow, maybe no wider than a pane of glass."

"It's a real nice theory, Arnold."

"That's what I mean when I say gravity may be the key to everything."

It took Vano a considerable while to formulate his response, and even then he wasn't sure it was on the subject: "*Ultimate hooommm* may mean particle people existence or belonging to the Federation," he said. "It might mean becoming blended with the entire electromagnetic spectrum."

"That's just the point," Arnold continued. "You can't talk about the electromagnetic spectrum without talking about gravity. If you have a black hole, it means the gravitational force is so strong that not even light can escape from it."

Vano didn't answer. Arnold got up from his bed so he could have a look over his roommate's shoulder. "Are you running a program?"

"No."

"What's this entry? How did you make this entry?"

It took some time. Eventually Vano explained, "I didn't enter it. The entry I made was just a list of book titles. More or less."

"You don't even have an active program. An entry can't just appear all by itself."

Vano told him, "The book titles just disappeared, like they erased themselves. Then the word *evolution* took their place."

"But I'm telling you this can't be. This is just the program manager because there's no active program. This had to come from somewhere."

Vano's long pause came as the preamble to his

response: "I think it was the particle people."
Arnold sat down on the closest chair. "I'll say this for you, Vano, when you get a theory you stay with it. I'm going to take some notes, so please don't go too fast."
"I never go fast," Vano reminded him. "The last thing the particle people told me was that I would not have a complete understanding of existence until I knew *ultimate hooommm*. When they said it to me, I didn't understand, but now I do. I think."
Even though he was writing furiously, Arnold didn't welcome the yawning delay which interrupted Vano's discourse. "Well don't stop now."
Vano needed a deep breath first. "The ego mode is just a stage of evolutionary development. It's just as primitive to the particle people as apes learning to walk upright and use their hands is to us. The particle mode is a much higher plane of evolution. In a way, it might be the supreme plane of evolution because it more or less completes a circle, back to the atoms and particles the world began with. I'm not sure about that part. But the particle mode and *ultimate hooommm* are the same thing; that's the part I've got figured out."
"Then why didn't they just tell you that the particle mode was the same thing as *ultimate hooommm?*"
This answer too, was a long time coming. "I think they didn't want to encourage me to strive for *ultimate hooommm*. If it works on the same principle as regular *hooommm*, the harder you try to get in it the less success you have. *Hooommm* is something you just have to let happen to you."
Arnold Beeker was trying to grow a mustache. He fingered the few scraggly hairs which bothered his upper lip before saying, "So tell me this. What good does it do to know that the particle mode is a high plane of evolution? It

takes millions of years to pass from one evolutionary phase to another."

No answer was forthcoming, so Arnold continued, "Let's say the human race advances to the particle mode four million years from now. We'll never see it, so what's the good of knowing it? No offense, Vano, I'm not putting down your theory."

Vano smiled. "No offense. I think it would be possible to achieve *ultimate hooommm* in our lifetime. The reason I think so is because some of the particle people had their origins on planets where the ego mode prevails. I sometimes think even I myself have been at the threshold, those times when the earth seems to wobble on its axis. It would probably take an extremely deep *hooommm* and a perfect set of conditions."

The suddenly-energized Arnold Beeker was on his feet again. "If we're going to talk conditions, then what we need is data. Are you with me, Vano?"

"I don't think so," Vano replied politely.

Arnold began pacing while wringing his hands. "I'm talking about the manuscript! If Revuelto's manuscript locates what he calls folds in the earth, we might be able to plug them into the right computer program and find out if they are really gravitational weak spots. Now do you see what I mean?"

Vano said quietly, "I think you're saying they might be points of unusual electromagnetic activity."

"Exactly." This had the feeling of a finer adventure even than exploring caves.

Vano asked him, "If we had Professor Revuelto's manuscript, where could we find the computer program we need?"

"Crevecouer wrote one that surveys gravitational force fields throughout our solar system. That might be too

limited, but maybe worth a try."
"How do you know about the Crevecouer program?"
"Vano, that's the kind of stuff I know about. Revuelto would never loan me his manuscript, though. I told him his theory about folds in the earth was off the track; I don't think he likes me."
"Maybe he would loan it to me," Vano offered.
"Well, you could always ask him," said Arnold.
"That's true. I could always ask him."

*

Oboe Meel's move from his own quarters to the academic dean's office positioned him to make two pleasant discoveries. To begin with, the office was so spacious that he could mount his dart board effectively. And in the second place, the new office, with floor-to-ceiling glass on the south and the west, provided a ready-made basking *ambience*.

It didn't take Oboe long to learn that he could avail himself of both pleasures at once. Bathing in refracted sunlight, he eased himself into his overstuffed chair. From this semi-recline, he could still launch darts at the target across the room. The only downside was retrieving the darts.

Today's target happened to be his new philosophy unit test, which consisted of two questions:

1. *Which is real: the blowfish inflated or deflated?*

2. *Let's say a meteor falls in a forest and crushes a slug to smithereens. What about that?*

He decided to determine the test's right answers by throwing darts at it. When he threw the first dart, it went straight down to lodge in the carpet, a few inches from his chair leg. "Okay, so it's been a long time," he muttered. "All this means is that I'm a little rusty."

He threw the second dart, which missed the test but stuck in the wall. Encouraged by this improvement, Oboe stood up so as to try a behind-the-back toss. The dart missed the wall entirely and sailed through the open office doorway. Professor Revuelto happened to be passing in the hall. The dart embedded itself securely in Revuelto's right temple.

He winced with pain but continued walking. He went straight to the office of the campus nurse. Nurse Berry was astonished when she got a look at Revuelto and his dart. "How did this ever happen?"

"I wish I knew."

The nurse eyeballed the dart from several angles. "There's probably a perfect puncture wound there," she declared. "There isn't much I can do for you. You'll need to go to the hospital for a tetanus shot."

"Naturally," said Revuelto irritably.

He decided to teach his class first, though, even with the dart sticking out of his head. As he spoke to the students he began to feel numb, almost like he was hooked up to an anaesthetic drip. He commenced to conjugate verbs at the blackboard, before he remembered that this was anthropology; he hadn't taught conversational Spanish in 20 years.

Adding to his disorientation was the vision of Mary Thorne. Leaning forward and crossing her legs in her front row seat. Her breasts were fairly spilling out of her yellow halter top. Short of breath, Revuelto instructed the class to to open the text to page 104 in order to begin reading the next chapter independently. He moved as carefully as possible in Mary's direction to ask her if she needed individual help.

As soon as Revuelto leaned over Mary's desk, his view inside the halter top was nearly total; his breathing difficulties intensified. For her part, Mary found Revuelto repellent. He was sweating and drooling. His breathing was so labored he sounded like he was trying to blow up a stubborn balloon. *And what about that stupid dart in his head?*

Sitting across from Mary was Rita Lieberman. Rita knew that Revuelto had no true educational objective in mind, but was maneuvering for a close-up look at Mary's melons. This knowledge filled Rita with resentment. Taking the six-inch nail file swiftly from her purse, she prepared to stab Mary with it. She plunged the nail file downward in a powerful backhand arc, but it stabbed into the professor by mistake. It penetrated one and one-half inches into the *rhomboideus major* muscle next to his shoulder blade.

Revuelto stood up straight before he turned white. With the dart in his temple and the nail file in his back, he ground his teeth together to keep from screaming.

Once again, he walked rapidly to Nurse Berry's office. The pain was excruciating and his head was swimming. Nurse Berry could offer him no new advice. She said, "This doesn't change a thing. You'll still have to go to the hospital for a tetanus shot."

Revuelto drove to the hospital emergency room. The E. R. nurse, a muscle-bound female with hairy forearms, was named Ms. Greve. Revuelto handed his note from Nurse Berry to her.

"This tetanus shot will have to be in your rear end,"

Nurse Greve informed Revuelto. "Drop your trousers."

Revuelto was red in the face and humiliated. "Naturally," he said, through clenched teeth. He dropped his pants. He stood still, facing the examination table.

Nurse Greve took a long and searching look at the nail file in his back. "This looks familiar," she observed. "This looks like the nail file that's been used to stab Mary Thorne. Is that possible?"

Humiliated and in intense pain, the professor seethed an answer: "Yes. I'd say it's even likely."

"No kidding."

"I am standing here with my pants down, in great pain. Would you please do what it is you have to do?"

But remembering the well-favored curvature of Mary Thorne's posterior, Nurse Greve was getting a little vertigo of her own. She licked her lips. "You mean this stabbing was intended for Mary Thorne?" she asked Revuelto.

Revuelto seethed again, "I assume it was. Yes."

"Then maybe she should be the one here getting the tetanus shot."

Revuelto was ready to turn and strangle her, but Nurse Greve plunged the needle into his buttocks.

Then she sat him on the exam table. She removed the dart from his temple and the nail file from his back. As soon as she cleaned both wounds, she bandaged them. She was still thinking fondly of Mary Thorne, all the while. "Maybe it would be a good idea if you sent Mary in for a tetanus shot as well," she suggested.

"What for?"

"It never hurts to be too careful, is all I'm saying."

Revuelto went directly back to the campus. His head hurt and his butt ached, but his back was the keenest misery of all. When he reached his office, he found Vano Lucas waiting for him. With supreme effort, the professor

squeezed his way behind his desk.
    Vano had never seen an office so cluttered. In addition to the three life-sized statues of naked Aztec warriors, which more or less defined the path to the desk, Revuelto's office contained the following items: two overstuffed chairs, two filing cabinets, a bronze statue of Simon Bolivar, a bust of Cervantes, a pink plaster-of-paris flamingo, a Looney Tunes train set, a pair of praying hands cast in pewter, a statue of the Blessed Virgin, a portrait of the pope, a portrait of Eva Peron in a two-piece swimsuit, a bronze wall figure of Quetzalcoatl, and a huge stainless steel crucifix.
    Revuelto was terse with him: "What do you want?"
    "I came to ask if I could borrow your book on folds in the earth," said Vano politely, using the phrasing he had rehearsed.
    Stiff with pain, Revuelto nonetheless discovered an urge to tidy up. He began moving things around. "I know you. You are in my anthropology class. You sit still in your seat in the back row, but never say a word."
    The depth of Vano's *hooommm* predicted a long delay. Revuelto's observations were accurate, but he couldn't think of a reason for confirming them. He finally said, "Yes, that's so."
    Revuelto was trying to heft the Aztec statues into the office closet. Each of the statues weighed 35 pounds. With much effort, the wounded professor managed to cram one in, but neither the second nor the third would fit. "Why did I buy *three* of these??" he blurted out.
    If it was a question intended for him, Vano couldn't think of what the answer might be. He wondered if he ought to be helping with the lifting of the statues.
    "What interest do you have in folds in the earth?" Revuelto asked him.

Vano replied, "It may be possible to locate *ultimate hooommm* in this lifetime."

"I don't have the slightest idea what you're talking about." Revuelto struggled some more with the statues. He pushed and pulled, he tugged and swore, but the closet would not accomodate them. "The book is not published yet," he said.

"I know it isn't published yet," said Vano. "I wonder if you might let me borrow the manuscript."

Revuelto was fatigued and hurting. He took out his handkerchief in order to wipe the sweat from the folds which circumscribed his chubby neck. "Now I know you. You are the boyfriend of Mary Thorne. You are the one."

It took Vano a few moments to form the reply. "Not exactly, I guess. Mary and I have never had a date, but she does get heat for me."

"*Madre de Dios*!! You *are* the one!" A return to dizziness intensified Revuelto's level of discomfort. No one guarded a more febrile lust for Mary Thorne than did he. He wrote fantasies about her, which he kept collected in a loose leaf notebook. He sent her anonymous, amorous sonnets through the mail. He mopped his brow once again while looking Vano over carefully. "Can it be that you are the one?"

"I'm not sure I understand. I would very much enjoy seeing your manuscript, though."

"You *are* the one. If I have what you want, and you have what I want, then we will make a deal. Life is like that- you scratch my back and I scratch yours." Revuelto put his handkerchief back in his pocket.

Vano didn't understand, but the professor continued: "In other words, you bring me Mary Thorne and I bring you the manuscript."

Vano wondered how you would bring one person to

another person. "I don't understand," he said again.
"Then let me repeat it: you bring me Mary, and I will bring you the manuscript."
Vano said, "I'm not sure what this means. I've never asked Mary for a favor before."
"Take it or leave it," said Revuelto curtly. He went into a three-point stance and tried to shoulder block the two stubborn statues into the closet. This effort failed. "Caramba!" he bellowed. He threw a roundhouse right which socked one of the statues on the jaw. The statue felt no pain, but Revuelto had just fractured the middle two fingers on his right hand.
Vano made a polite suggestion, "If you would like to give one of the statues away, I think I know someone who would enjoy having it."
"You do?"
It was at this moment that Rita Lieberman came into view. She said to Revuelto, "I came to apologize for stabbing you."
"This is an amazing coincidence," Vano observed. "Rita is the person I had in mind. I think she might enjoy having one of your statues."
"I swear it was an accident," said Rita. "It was the bitch who was supposed to get it, not you. You can probably imagine how sorry I am."
The wounded professor couldn't imagine much of anything. He was listening to Rita through waves of pain. "I bear no grudge," he told her. "If you would like a statue, please help yourself."
"You serious?" Rita Lieberman took a long and lingering look at the imposing dimensions of the rigid member on each statue. "I wonder if they're all the same size. Never mind, close enough. I have a powerful sexual appetite, and I've never been shy about a kink or two every

now and then."

"You are welcome to have one," Revuelto repeated.

"You know what," said Rita, "If I did have one of these dudes, I'd probably keep it waxed with paste wax. I'd probably give the pecker a second coat. I might even give that part a *buff job*, if you get my drift."

Revuelto gasped his way down to a seated position on the floor. He was about to faint beneath the acuity of his accumulated wounds and frustrations. "Do you have a car?" he asked Rita.

"I don't just have a car, I have a Vette."

"I think I have a broken hand. Would you be so kind as to drive me to the hospital?"

"Hey--it's the least I can do." She swung one of the Aztecs up onto her shoulder before heading on down the hallway. Revuelto followed at a close distance. Vano watched them until they became very small. Rita's right hand had a firm grip on the statue's pecker.

*

When the phone on Arnold's desk rang, it was for Vano. It was Sister Cecilia, calling from the main desk downstairs. She told Vano, "There's something urgent I have to talk to you about."

Vano went on down, where he found Sister pacing in the lounge. She looked around. "Your dormitory is nice, Vano. I'm glad you have such a nice place to be."

After a pause he responded by saying, "The dorm is very nice."

"I have some awful news, Vano. I thought it would be better if I came here to tell you in person." Her large brown eyes were round and liquid.

Vano sat down beside her on the sofa nearest to the window. "What is the news?"

"I don't really know how to tell you this. Your father died this morning of a sudden heart attack."

Vano receded into deeper *hooommm*. There was orange lava roiling outside the window.

Sister Cecilia continued, "I don't think he suffered, Vano. He was dead on arrival at the hospital."

When Vano finally found his tongue, he asked her, "How did it happen?"

"I never did understand exactly what it was they were trying to tell me," said Sister. "They said he burned himself on hot coffee in a restaurant, which caused him to have the heart attack."

Vano said nothing.

"I don't know how you could get a heart attack from a cup of coffee, but it's what they told me, honest."

Sister Cecilia had the Lincoln. Right after Vano packed a few of his things, they headed back to the condo. Vano spent the next two days deep in, sitting on the balcony. Sister wrote a lot of notes and did a lot of telephoning.

On the third day, there was a graveside service in the cemetery. Two old men who had been business partners of his father were the only mourners besides Vano and Sister. Not even Gomez or Ann-Marie showed up.

The minister, who wore a black hat and a black suit, prepared to read from a black book. He began his speech by saying, "Our Heavenly Father, we are gathered here to honor thy servant, Vernon Lucas, who walked the path of righteousness all his days."

Vano's *hooommm* was the deepest he'd ever known. The earth shook like a subway in motion while his ears roared. The orange lava rising in all directions nearly formed an overhead canopy. Was this the *Federation*? Was he standing at the threshold of *ultimate hooommm*? He didn't hear the rest of the minister's words. Instead, he stared at his mother's headstone, only a few feet away from the fresh-dug, open grave. It wasn't so long ago that Ann-Marie had given him a blow job on this very spot. The memory was clear in its details, but void of emotional content. It was neutral.

When the minister was finished with his remarks, it was time to lower the casket into the grave, but the grave was a tad too small. The gravediggers tried to force in into place with their feet, but the casket thoroughly wedged itself to the sides of the opening. One end of the casket was higher than the other. They covered it with dirt anyway, but when they were done, the dirt formed a peculiar, uneven mound, unlike any other grave in the cemetery.

"It doesn't matter, Vano," Sister reassured him. "The position of the casket isn't important. He's with the Lord now, which is the only thing that really matters."

"The casket will be fine," said Vano.

In the middle of the night, Vano awoke from a sound sleep to find Sister Cecilia standing next to his bed. He pulled himself slowly into a sitting position. "Are we going to put your nightgown on now?" he asked her.

"Vano, can't you see my nightgown is already on? I just need someone to talk to. Everything is so up in the air."

"Of course."

The two of them lay on their backs side by side. Vano liked the smell of Sister's skin and hair, as well as her baby powder. But he was located in a *hooommm* that was ever so solid.

"I've been going through lots of your father's things. Old files and records--those kind of things."

"That's a good subject, Sister. I've been meaning to

ask you a favor. Please send ten thousand dollars to a friend of mine named Herne Hill. He's trying to start up a franchise business."

"I see."

"He's at the *Arbors,* but I don't think he'll be there too much longer. You can send the money to him there."

"Of course, Vano. I'll send it first thing in the morning." Then she told him that she missed his father. "Do you think you'll miss him too, Vano?"

Vano had to think. A long time. Finally he said, "I doubt it."

"I know you and your father didn't see eye to eye, but he's dead now."

"My father always treated me like an unperson," said Vano.

"But please, he's dead now, and we pray he's at rest with the Lord. You mustn't carry a grudge."

"I don't have any grudge," Vano explained. "There are no grudges in *hooommm.* I think it was important that my father treated me as an unperson. The reality may be, you can't experience *hooommm* without first becoming an unperson."

"I'm just not sure sometimes, the things you say."

"Me neither."

Sister Cecilia rolled on her side to face him. Her mouth was six inches from his left ear, and the top of her nightgown was open. Vano took note of the dormant condition of her large brown nipples, but his zone was undisturbed. "Vano, I'm not sure what to do. What's to become of me?"

He asked her what she meant.

"I've spent the last five years taking care of you and your father. Mostly your father. He always needed more looking after than you. I've spent the last five years cooking, cleaning, washing, ironing, keeping the checkbook balanced, shopping, running errands, and making sure Vernon remembered to take his medicine."

Vano didn't reply.

Sister continued. "What I'm saying is, everything's so up in the air. I'm not sure what to do with myself. I don't know the Lord's will yet. It's not a good time for me to be alone, so do you suppose I could come and stay with you for a while?"

"Sure," said Vano. "That would be nice."

"I promise it wouldn't be for too long," she said. "Just till I figure out what the Lord has in mind for me."

"I'm sure it would be real nice to have you, Sister."

The following day, Sister Cecilia took one small suitcase and her trombone. She moved into the dorm with Vano, Robin, and Arnold. They set up an army cot for her at the north end of the room. She had only a few personal belongings, and Vano was more than happy to share his closet space with her.

The first day after Sister took up residence, Mrs. Kuetemeyer stopped her as she was passing the main desk. "Hold it there just a minute," said Mrs. Kuetemeyer. "I'd like to know what you have in the case."

"This is my trombone," Sister explained. "I play it in a Salvation Army band. I hope I haven't been disturbing you."

"I've been missing a Commodore personal computer for several weeks now. How do I know the computer is not in that case?"

Sister Cecilia smiled. "This is a trombone case. I doubt if a computer would fit inside it."

"If you have nothing to hide, I don't suppose you'd mind if I opened it up to take a look?" asked Mrs. Kuetemeyer.

"You're welcome to open the case."

Mrs. Kuetemeyer opened the case and considered the shiny trombone. She said, "Okay, but how do I know you can play it?"

As soon as Sister played a few bars of *Bringing in the Sheaves,* Mrs. Kuetemeyer admitted she was satisfied. She even apologized.

Apart from this one incident, the pattern of Sister Cecilia's residency could not have been any smoother. She spent most of her time in prayer. She only practiced her trombone at noon, when the likelihood of disturbing people was remote. All the guys in the dorm enjoyed taking showers with her. She did laundry every day for Vano and his roommates, and she kept the room dusted with lemon Pledge.

*

The very first words out of Mrs. Askew's mouth were, "I'm afraid I'm going to have to give you another reminder about curriculum development. It's truly an urgent situation."

Reggie Rose was peeved. *Was this any way to greet a president?* "Whatever happened to 'good morning?'" he asked. "Or possibly, 'have a nice day?'"

"Good morning and have a nice day. Did you hear what I said?"

"Yes, yes, I heard you. There's nothing wrong with my memory." He headed into his own office where he plopped down behind his desk. Mrs. Askew followed him expectantly. Reggie decided that she was just as gratuitous as she was officious. "Where's the dean?" he asked her.

"Where's the academic dean?"

"Do you really need to ask?"

Reggie began to pout. "I suppose this means I'll have to find the astrology teacher on my own."

"It looks that way," Mrs. Askew confirmed. She chomped her gum.

"But I'm the one who thought it up in the first place!" exclaimed the president. "What can I delegate?"

Mrs. Askew had no answer. She assumed this was a rhetorical question and anyway, she was using her compact mirror to remove a lipstick stain from one of her front teeth.

"Egad!" Reggie wailed. "My work load is awesome! It is *crushing*!"

"It is lonely at the top," observed the secretary, just before leaving.

Reggie stood up to pace. First he paced right, then to the left. He couldn't imagine where a person would look to find an astrology teacher. He racked his brain, but all he could think of was Bertie Kerfoot's annoying bridge party from the night before. He experienced a fresh wave of dejection.

Additional pacing and extended brain-wracking got him nowhere. He went to Mrs. Askew's office. "Do you have the morning paper?" he asked.

"Right here. But don't do anything to the crossword."

Reggie took the newspaper to his desk. He began his search in the classifieds, piecing through the various headings: *Real Estate. Employment. Automotive. Garage Sales.* Then, under the boldface heading **Services Offered**, he happened upon the most intriguing item:

ARCANE EXPRESS--astrology, scientology, palms,

phrenology, I Ching, Ying and Yang, ping and pong, cheech and chong, rosicrucian rites, llamaism, crystal balls, bones. If it's weird, we probably do it. No waiting. Call today for an appointment.

Reggie picked up the phone hastily to dial the number.

The man who answered the phone said simply, "Arcane."

Reggie introduced himself. He said he needed a teacher for an introductory course in astrology. He also said that Entrada was committed to developing an entire curriculum in astrology sometime in the near future.

The man on the other end said, "I can teach the course, Man."

"Are you sure?" Reggie asked. "I should tell you that it only pays one thousand dollars."

"A thousand bucks? I'm real sure."

"What's your name?" asked the president.

"Herne Hill" was the answer.

Did he say Herne Hill? Reggie asked himself. "Did you say your name was Herne Hill?"

"That's what I said, Man."

"See here. Can you come to my office sometime next week for an interview?"

"Count on it."

Relieved and proud, Reggie Rose hung up the phone. Not only was he setting the college back on the path to Godliness, he was also leading the way in curriculum development. Enthusiastically, he pounded his fist on his desk.

Then Mrs. Askew appeared in his doorway. She declared, "A wealthy alum named Wilfong Weingrad just called. He wants to give the college 25 million dollars."

Before he could respond, Reggie needed to catch his

breath. "Did I hear you say 25 million? Is that what you said?"
"That's what I said."
"This is incredible. 25 million dollars would put us back on a firm financial foundation. I hope you told him we accept?"
"I did, but he's got terms."
"Terms?"
"Terms." said Mrs. Askew. "First, the college has to construct a chapel in his honor, in the center of campus. Second, the college has to bring an evangelical preaching crusade to campus."
Reggie was quick to put his enthusiasm on hold. "You mean like Billy Graham or Oral Roberts?"
"I think that's the general idea."
"Tell me something," said Reggie. "What made him decide to give us all this money?"
"He saw one of our chaplain's memos," she replied. "The one about God floating through the heavens."
"I see. Mrs. Askew, with these resources, I think Entrada may be on the road to a complete recovery. More than that, I think we may be standing on the threshold of a new age. What do you think?"
"I think you'd better call the bank."
"Explain yourself."
"I think you'd better call the bank and make sure he's got the money. I've seen Wilfong Weingrad once or twice. I doubt if his elevator goes all the way to the top."
It was necessary for Reggie to put his enthusiasm on hold again. He stood up to resume his pacing. "Mrs. Askew, let's get the ball rolling. I'll call the bank. You get the chaplain over here ASAP."
As soon as Mrs. Askew left the room, Reggie called the bank. He asked a bank officer if Wilfong Weingrad

really did have the money. The bank officer reported that Weingrad had 2500 passbook savings accounts in the amount of ten thousand dollars each.

"Why does he do it that way?" Reggie asked. "Why doesn't he have his fortune invested in a portfolio?"

"Have you ever met Weingrad?"

"No," Reggie admitted.

"Then don't ask," said the bank officer.

But Reggie had to know, "Why are you giving me all this information about his financial holdings over the phone? Isn't that a violation or something?"

"Yes." was the reply. "It is a violation. It's just so weird, I can't help telling people about it."

After Reggie hung up the phone, Chaplain Johansen arrived. The chaplain was carrying his briefcase.

Reggie beckoned the chaplain to a chair and proclaimed, "I have an important mission for you."

Johansen sat down. "For me? You do?"

"A very wealthy alumnus named Wilfong Weingrad saw your memo about God floating through the heavens," the president informed him. "He was very taken with it."

"He was?"

"That's not all. Weingrad has 25 million dollars which he will give to Entrada if he's convinced that this is a place with an appropriate fear of the Lord."

Chaplain Johansen whistled his appreciation. "That's a lot of money."

"You ain't just a-woofin'. And believe you me, this college could use the resources. I could show you in the trustees' report, but right now we don't have the time."

The president's sense of urgency was making Chaplain Johansen nervous. "What is it you would like me to do?"

"I'm appointing you liaison," Reggie informed him.

"I'm sending you out to secure the 25 million."

"I see," murmured the chaplain. "No I don't, what does that mean?"

"It means our friend Weingrad has some terms we will have to meet. I'm putting you in charge. First of all, we're going to have to build a chapel in his honor."

"I see."

"Second, we are going to have to bring a preaching crusade to campus. One of those evangelists. Who do you think we should pick?"

The chaplain had no ready answer for this. He worried his rosary beads before he said, "I'm afraid I don't know much about evangelistic crusades."

"You're the chaplain, aren't you? You must have some resources."

"Well," said Johansen, "I have a few catalogues here." He opened his briefcase so he could hand Reggie one of the evangelical catalogues.

Reggie flipped some of the pages rapidly before he frowned. "What's this card for?" he asked.

"That's one of the easy-order coupons. You get a discount if you use it."

Reggie was a little nonplussed by this approach. "Can you order an evangelist just like you would order a pair of trail boots from L.L. Bean?"

"It would appear that way," said the chaplain, "But I really don't know very much about these things."

By this point, Reggie Rose was tired of the whole subject. He did not want to think any more about the Wilfong Weingrad chapel or the evangelists. In fact, he didn't want to think about college business at all. "You pick someone," he said wearily. "I'm sure you'll do fine." With that, he dismissed the chaplain.

Johansen went back to his office. He turned

catalogue pages from cover to cover, but it was disorienting. He didn't seem able to make a choice. It wasn't anything you could crank out on the mimeo machine. As a last resort, he threw one of the catalogues up in the air, to see how it might land; he seemed to remember choosing scripture lessons by this method. The catalogue fell open to Billy Joe Jim Bob of Tupelo, Mississippi.

Chapter Seven

The night that Vano had his date with Mary Thorne, he decided to drive the Town Car. First, though, he had to remove the many parking tickets from the windshield in order to drive.

At the Kappa sorority, Mary met him on the porch. She approved of the vehicle: "Nice car. Very nice." She was wearing a sleeveless, lemon colored linen sheath. The dress had a deep, square neckline with a white lace border. Mary was also wearing white button earrings, white bangle bracelets on each arm, and white pumps. Her manicured nails glistened with a frosted polish. Vano Lucas felt that he had never seen a woman so stunning, and in truth, he never had.

"So where are we going?" she asked.

Even though he was in solid, he felt the slightest trace of nerves. He was wearing a black suit, a white dress shirt, and a thin black tie which he had borrowed from Arnold Beeker. He finally said, "I'm very fond of cheeseburgers. How about McDonald's?"

"McDonald's? You've got to be kidding."

"Maybe we could try Hardee's."

"You expect me to go for the Big Mac dressed like this?"

"Well, we could go anyplace you like, actually."

"Jesus Christ, come with me. If I'm going to the arches, I need to change first."

She took Vano up to her room, where she immediately began removing her clothes. Concurrently, she delivered Vano some new information. "My father is coming down here tomorrow. He wants to be here for parents' weekend."

"That's real nice, Mary."

"That's what you think. He's going to take me to some seminar at the Holiday Inn on starting up worm farms. My father is always starting up a new company of some kind. When I graduate, he wants to make me executive vice president in charge of *worm farms*. Can you believe it?"

Mary was now removing her underthings. Vano asked her why.

"There is dress up underwear, and there is dress down underwear. You've probably never thought about that, have you?"

"No, Mary, I never have. I've never thought about worm farms either. I don't know anything about them."

"Who does? Who cares?" Now completely nude, she asked a third rhetorical question: "With a body like this, do I belong behind a desk running a worm farm?"

Vano stared at the shapes and textures of her exquisite body. It occurred to him that he ought to be experiencing a chain reaction of anatomical changes, but he found that he rested in a solid *hooommm* which was nearly unaffected. He didn't even have a stiff. He changed the subject by saying, "I've been looking into changing my major, like you and I talked about. They're going to have astrology now."

"Astrology? You mean like horoscopes and that kind of stuff?"

"I'm pretty sure. But I don't think you can sign up for it until next semester or next year."

"That figures. As soon as it's time for me to graduate, they start having all the good courses."

They went to McDonald's. Mary was now attired in a Santa Barbara sweatshirt, designer blue jeans, and white sandals of patent leather. She ordered a Big Mac, regular fries, and medium Dr. Pepper. Vano had the same, except a cheeseburger instead of the Big Mac.

Vano began by saying, "I'm real glad you told me about the worm farm, Mary. It helps me to get to know you better."

"Didn't you hear what I said? He can wait till Hell freezes over before I have anything to do with a worm farm!" She slid three fries into her mouth.

Vano decided it would be a good idea to change the subject. After a pause he said, "Mary, I'd like to ask a favor."

"So go ahead."

"I'd like to borrow a manuscript which belongs to Professor Revuelto. I talked to him last week. He said he won't give it to me, but he'll give it to you."

"What is that supposed to mean?"

"I'm not one hundred percent sure," said Vano. "I think his exact words were, 'you bring me Mary Thorne and I bring you the manuscript.'"

"Oh Jesus."

"Like I said, I'm not completely sure what it means."

"Well I am," Mary declared. "I know exactly what it means. He sends me this kinky stuff in the mail; he thinks I don't know where it comes from. He wants me to come out to his house and take my clothes off so he can take erotic Polaroids."

"I see," said Vano.

"As if. He wants me naked so he can give me a rubdown with a mink glove, while he reads his pissy poems to me."

"I see."

"The bottom line is, Revuelto's a pervert sweathog. What is this book that you want from him?"

"It's a book about folds in the earth," Vano explained. "It isn't published yet. I want to borrow it because my roommate and I would like to do some computations on the electromagnetic spectrum and possible fissures in the gravitational field."

"I'm sure I don't know what you're talking about," said Mary. She began eating her sandwich.

Vano hesitated before speaking. "You now what, Mary? I should take my own advice. If you and I are going to get to know each other better, I should tell you something about myself."

Her mouth was full: "If it works for you."

Summarizing as carefully but efficiently as he could, Vano told Mary about *hooommm*. Then he told her about his visit with the particle people, and reviewed what they had revealed to him. He explained the difference between the particle mode and the ego mode. He pointed out how the ego mode was just a primitive phase of psychological evolution, much like the flexible thumb represented a different kind of evolutionary phase. He concluded by outlining how he surmised that *ultimate hooommm* was none other than the particle mode itself.

Mary Thorne's mouth was open, in the shape of an O. "How long were you in that looney bin, anyway?"

Vano smiled. "About ten days."

"Did I say you were dull?"

"Not really, Mary, you just said that I wasn't very interesting."

Mary turned back to her fries and soft drink.

"There's one other point that's kind of interesting, Mary. People like us, living here on earth, will probably never get to a higher plane of psychological development. That's because even though our technology is advanced, our ego mode is primitive. We will blow ourselves up, one way or another, and sort of go back to the stone age. I figure that's the way it's happened on lots of planets for eons. Wherever there's a humanoid life form. The technological advancement comes a lot faster because of the ego mode, but it's the same ego mode that prevents control and judgment. There's never enough time for the humanoids to reach a higher plane of evolution; they always have to go back to the beginning and start over. Anyway, that's my basic conclusion on the meaning of existence. Of course it really isn't mine at all, since it comes from the particle people."

Mary was finished eating. She said, "I don't have any cigarettes. They sell them in the Convenience store. How'd you like to go get me a pack?"

"Sure, I'd be glad to."

"I take Marlboro Lites."

The Convenience store was only across the parking lot, so Vano was back in no time at all. Mary lit up right away, then blew a wobbly smoke ring toward the ceiling. "Look," she began. "You're a good kid, and you're not dull like I said. I don't know where you're coming from, though. I know what *getting heat* is."

Of course, Vano thought to himself. Sometimes in *hooommm* meanings just fell into place like jigsaw puzzles. *Getting heat* was to Mary what *hooommm* was to him. *Of course.* But he didn't say anything, he simply chewed on his ice.

"I'll tell you what," Mary suggested. "The heat is gone, but maybe one for the road would be nice. Did you ever do it standing up?"

Vano tried to remember by thinking of Ann-Marie. "I can't say for sure, but I think maybe I have."

"Okay then, how about this? Did you ever do it in a football stadium?"

"No."

"Neither have I. See? There's something we have in common. About this Revuelto thing, I'm not making any promises. I'm not saying I will, but I'm not saying I won't. It might not be any worse than going to a seminar on worm farms."

"You'll think it over then?" Vano asked.

"I'll think it over. You did bring the heat, but I'm still not making any promises."

"That's fair enough, Mary."

"How about one for the road in the football stadium, standing up?"

"That would be real nice, Mary."

They tried sexual intercourse in the end zone, first standing up and then lying down in the grass. It didn't work either way, though, because Vano couldn't establish a sufficient erection. As ravishing as she was, he couldn't find enough focus. They finally gave it up when Mary said, "Jesus Christ, this never happened to me before."

Vano knew he wouldn't be seeing Mary any more. He wondered if he would miss her. But he didn't see Ann-Marie anymore, and he hardly missed her at all. "Actually, Mary, it isn't happening to you. It's happening to me."

"That's easy for you to say. I never thought this could happen to me."

"It's just my zone," said Vano, in a loud voice. He was entering a *hooommm* as deep as any he'd ever known. Orange lava elevated in the darkness above the stadium on all sides. It formed a textured, layered canopy.

When Mary said something about a blow to her self-esteem, her distant voice was swallowed by the deep, rumbling roar and intense vibration. He might have told her *that's one of the pitfalls of ego mode existence*, but he felt suspended out of his own body while the earth wobbled precariously on its axis. Suddenly, she seemed so far away

and so long ago.
Vano thought he might be passing over into *ultimate hooommm*, leaving all the world as he knew it behind.
He wasn't, though. When the deep zone finally ebbed, he was still beneath the goal posts. It was dawn, and Mary was gone.

*

The middle of the following week, President Rose summoned Chaplain Johansen. The timid cleric arrived carrying stacks of printed material.
The impatient president wasn't inclined to beat around the bush: "Tell me where we stand on this evangelistic preaching mission stuff."
Chaplain Johansen cleared his throat. "I've filled out an order form on Billy Joe Jim Bob of Tupelo, Mississippi."
"Is he any good?"
"I have no idea."
"How much does he cost?"
"I have no idea. He has four first names."
"Is that good?"
"I have no idea."
Reggie was frustrated; he felt like that ought to be enough conversation about traveling preachers. "Let's move along to the Wilfong Weingrad chapel."
Johansen opened his briefcase and began removing material. He had been to see the famous architect, Prosper Tornquist. Prosper Tornquist had drawn up a few preliminary sketches, which the chaplain showed to Reggie.
The Tornquist proposal was to build a 1:2 scale replica of Westminster Abbey. His drawings called for

vaulted ceilings, flying buttresses, countless leaded, stained glass windows, chandeliers of crystal, and a huge stone altar of Purbeck marble. There was to be carving and statuary throughout the building. "Isn't this sublime?" Johansen asked.

But as soon as President Rose absorbed the implications of these drawings, he was appalled. "This is preposterous!"

"You don't like it?"

Reggie decided outrageous would be a good word. "This is outrageous! We would spend almost every penny of the 25 million dollars just building this chapel!"

"Is that bad?"

"It's worse than bad. Read the trustees' report sometime if you don't believe me. We need money to upgrade the physical facilities, the curriculum, and the faculty." Having said this, Reggie got out *his* sketch for the Weingrad chapel. This drawing had been prepared the previous evening, by Bertie Kerfoot, in a state of advanced inebriation. It was drawn on a grocery bag with egg salad grease stains.

The Bertie Kerfoot drawing called for a ten by twenty foot building of two-by-four studs and grade B exterior plywood. It was to be painted with red barn paint, which could be purchased for 25 dollars per five gallon bucket. It was to be roofed with tar paper and tin. It was to have a front door, a back door, and two 30-inch windows.

"This building can be constructed for 2600 dollars!" beamed the president.

"It's awfully small," Chaplain Johansen felt obliged to point out.

"So? Nobody ever goes to chapel services anyway, you told me so yourself."

"That's true. But it doesn't have any religious

symbols in it. I don't think it would be very inspirational. It doesn't have any heat or bathrooms, either."

Reggie Rose waved his hand. "We can worry about the fine print later on." He was fatigued in the extreme by this entire conversation. "You need to get yourself up to Salinas to ferret out Weingrad's estate. Show him your own sketches if he wants a look at some kind of prospectus. You probably won't have to, though; just let him do most of the talking."

"How will I get there?"

"His home is located in a rather remote spot, I'm told. You'll probably need a road map."

"I don't have a road map," the chaplain explained.

"Then you'll have to get one, won't you?"

"I don't have a car, either."

"Egad, Man! You'll have to take charge! Must I be responsible for everyone's sphere of duty?" He dismissed the chaplain summarily.

*

When Vano returned to the dorm on Monday, following his philosophy class, Arnold was waiting for him. "Mary Thorne was here a little while ago," was the information Arnold provided. "She brought Revuelto's manuscript."

"That's nice."

"It's more than nice, Vano, a lot more. It's exactly what we need."

"It's very nice."

"How did she talk Revuelto into giving her the manuscript?" Arnold wanted to know.

"There's no telling. Mary is very persuasive, especially when it comes to men."

Robin Snook burst out laughing. He was lying on his bed, lighting farts, and reading from a *Far Side Gallery* collection of cartoons. Arnold Beeker was trying to ignore him. He told Vano, "It was in that large manilla envelope over there. I hope you don't mind, but I went ahead and opened it."

"I don't mind," said Vano. He sat down to take a look at the manuscript. It consisted of 340 typed pages, in a neat stack. "This would be nice to read."

"I've been thumbing through it," said Arnold. "It's all in there. All the places are named. What I have to do now is calculate latitudes and longitudes and then plug them into Professor Crevecouer's program."

After a few seconds, Vano asked, "Shall we do it now?"

Arnold took off his glasses in order to adjust the adhesive tape which secured the frames. "I wish it was that easy. Crevecouer's program is stored in the computer in the registrar's office. If we're going to do this, we have to access that system."

"Perhaps we should just use your computer," Vano suggested.

"Impossible. This is only an IBM compatible. It doesn't have near enough memory. The computer in the registrar's office is a huge mainframe."

Robin Snook burst out laughing again. "Check this out," he said. He showed them a cartoon of two amoebas playing poker and complaining about their hands. Vano laughed, but Arnold was annoyed.

"With all due respect," he told Robin, "I'm trying to get something accomplished here."

Robin cut a noisy fart and then blew cigar smoke into

Arnold's face. "You need to lighten up," was his advice.

Vano asked Arnold, "What would we have to do to run Professor Crevecouer's program?"

"We would have to access that system through this computer." Arnold was using Kleenex to dab at his eyes, which were tearing from the cigar smoke.

Vano was receding into a much deeper *hooommm*. He stared at the monitor, where the screen saver took the form of a flexing thumb moving horizontally at a slow pace. After several seconds he said, "I think we should try." Saying this, he bumped the mouse.

"Try what? This is just my program manager, there's not even any application active. God knows what all we would need; probably a password and maybe even a user ID."

Arnold was now a blip. Vano could hear him, but just above a distant muffled roar like a constant stormy ocean. After another lengthy pause he said, "Please use the key number. The computer will ask us questions and we'll see if we have the answers."

"Have the answers?"

"I mean maybe the answers will come to us."

Arnold shrugged his shoulders. "You want me to type words on a program manager, not using any application. Okay, Buddy Boy, just check this out." But to his amazement, Arnold discovered the letters he typed appeared on the screen, clear and bold. First, he shook his head several times in disbelief, then he went ahead and typed *Access Fileserver Entrada Reg. 1* on the monitor.

"What's that?" Vano asked.

"That's the access code to the mainframe," Arnold informed him. When the new instructions appeared on the monitor, *Please Enter User Identification,* Arnold's disorientation escalated; he couldn't fathom the first development, so how would he come to terms with this one? "This can't be happening."

"I think we should enter *opposable thumb*," said Vano.

"*Opposable thumb? Why not macaroni and cheese or coney dogs with onion?* I mean, this is all nuts anyway, it can't be happening."

"I think it's important."

"No offense, Vano, but you're talking to a program manager and getting answers! That's not the way it works. I could tell you about the user ID problem and the password that's probably involved, but none of this makes sense in the first place!"

Vano was sorry to see his friend so nonplussed. He smiled patiently before he said, "Please enter it, Arnold; can it do any harm to try?"

"Okay, okay, it can't hurt to try. Just remember, I'm only doing this to make you happy." Arnold typed *Opposable thumb* on the screen in crisp Helvetica letters. A few moments passed before the screen delivered a response:

Thank you.

Arnold Beeker shook his head before he got to his feet. "I have to go to the john," he said.

He was gone for a few minutes but when he returned, he was still shaking his head. "I don't understand any of this, Vano; this is downright scary."

Vano smiled. He couldn't feel any fear. Laughing out loud, Robin approached again to share another cartoon. This one showed dinosaurs behind the barn, sneaking cigarettes. "This is how the dinosaurs became extinct; get it?"

"I get it," Vano said. Then he told Arnold, "I think

you should run the program now."

"Vano, you can't do this. This is not how systems work."

"Would you please try it, Arnold?"

Arnold gave up and tried. He typed *Run Starpul*. Vano asked, "What's that?"

"That's the name of Crevecouer's program."

"How do you know that?"

"It's the kind of thing I know, Vano; you might give me a little credit."

At this point, *Please Enter Password* appeared on the screen.

This was Vano's prompt to say, "I think the password is *hooommm*."

A password can't just be the first thing that pops into your mind. Besides that, nobody knows about hoom but you."

"Actually, I'm not the first person to locate in *hooommm*. Not by a long shot. The particle people were quite clear about that."

"But I'm trying to tell you how these systems work."

Looking up from his cartoon collection, Robin interrupted: "Goddamit, I'm tryin' to concentrate here. Do what he says, or I might have to coldcock you."

Arnold swallowed before he said, "Okay, already. I'll enter it."

"Please be sure you spell it right," Vano cautioned. "That's three o's and three m's."

"I'll remember," Arnold said meekly. He entered *hooommm*. Immediately the screen responded:

Loading Starpul

"We're in," Arnold announced. "I'm sorry, but I

can't believe what's going on here. Vano, where do these things come from?"

"I think they don't come from me," Vano replied. "It must be that they come from the particle people."

"Scarier and scarier," Arnold declared. "It's like you have a pipeline straight to God or something."

Vano took the time to remind him, "Don't forget what the particle people teach about God. The kind of God most people perceive doesn't exist. There is the universe expanding and contracting. There are the waves and there are the particles."

"This is no time for theology, Vano. I've spent years thinking up theories and then calculating the probabilities. One of my best theories is how the earth is actually an egg. Have I ever told you that one?"

"No, Arnold, I don't think you ever have."

Robin Snook groaned. He was eating from a large bag of pretzels. "I think what Vano meant to say is we've heard that theory before."

Arnold ignored him. "The earth is a huge egg, and what we call the atmosphere is reallly an enormous membrane. It will take some cataclysmic event, such as nuclear war, to crack the membrane. That's how the egg gets hatched."

"It's a real nice theory, Arnold."

"That's too brief a summary to really do it justice, but here's what I'm saying to you: theories are theories, but what you're doing is too real. It could even have real *consequences*. Do you see what I'm getting at?"

If he listened very carefully, Vano could hear Arnold's voice where it penetrated his field of orange vibrations. He looked at Arnold down the long orange tunnel before he said, "Since we've come this far, maybe we should start running some data."

"We might as well," Arnold admitted. "It seems like we're in the program."

Then there was a knock at the door. Vano opened it to find Herne Hill standing on the threshold with John in tow. "Lllllllll," said John. Herne was carrying his french horn beneath his arm. "Hot damn, *amigo*! So soon we meet again!"

Vano said, "This is a pleasant surprise, Herne."

"Life's a beach, ain't it?" Herne Hill entered the room. He gave Arnold Beeker a whack on the back, then exchanged a high five with Robin. He gave Vano the good news: "I'm on a roll, *compadre*! I'm here for an interview with your president so I can teach a course in astrology. Besides that, the *Arcane Express* is off the ground. I got ten thousand bucks through the mail for start-up money! Am I on a roll, or what?!"

Vano smiled. Robin asked, "Who gave you the money?"

"I'm not sure," said Herne. "The letter wasn't signed. It was written on Salvation Army stationery, so I guess it must've been them." Then he announced that he had five thousand fliers printed up for advertising. Robin wanted to know how he intended to circulate them.

"I ain't got a clue."

"You leave those babies to me," said Robin. He took a look at his watch, which had a calendar. "My suspension is up in just a few days. I'll leaflet your fliers from the sky."

"This is outrageous!" exclaimed Herne. "When you're hot, you're hot!" Robin offered Herne some pretzels and a cold can of Coors Light.

Arnold was tearing off segments of computer printout, inspecting them, then tossing them into the waste basket. With his mouth full of pretzels, Herne asked him

what he was doing.
 As briefly as he could, Arnold summarized the project.
 "So how's it going?" asked Hill.
 "So far, not too well. I don't have the right framework in place yet. I'm still in the preliminary stages. This is going to take a lot of gray matter. I can only hope I'm up to it."
 "Have you accounted for harmonic convergence?" Hill asked him.
 Arnold drew a blank. "Have I accounted for what?"
 "Harmonic convergence. You can't really talk about gravitational deviations without including the energy caused by the alignment of the planets. Know what I mean?" Herne stuffed six pretzels into his mouth, then washed them down with a long swallow of brew.
 "I'm not exactly sure what you mean," said Arnold. "Please continue."
 Herne belched loudly before he said, "On August 16, nine of our planets were aligned in a configuration called a grand trine. This phenomenon resulted in major energy all over the globe, which converged and harmonized with itself."
 "That's interesting," said Arnold politely, "but that was three months ago."
 Herne opened a second beer before he continued. "True, it's too late for the grand trine, but there are elliptical trines. There will be elliptical trines from time to time throughout this calendar year."
 "There's not much of the calendar year left," said Arnold. "Where would I find the data?"
 "It's all in a book by Arguelles called *The Mayan Factor*. He's got it all calculated, even down to the details in the Aztec and Mayan calendars. If I had my copy with me,

I'd be glad to loan it to you."

This information accelerated Arnold Beeker's enthusiasm. He turned to Vano, "You know what, Vano, what Herne is saying could be crucial to our project. With Revuelto's manuscript and Crevecouer's program, what we're targeting is *place*. Herne is pointing out that we need to establish the *time* factor as well."

Vano was in deep and comfortable. He said, "I think it sounds real nice."

Arnold found this remark inadequate. "Is that all you can say?"

Vano added, "I could check the Arguelles book out of the library if it would help."

"You probably could, but we may be on the verge of a monumental discovery here. At least you could show a little enthusiasm."

Vano smiled before he pointed out, "Conventional enthusiasm is not a part of *hooommm*. It's a very level place."

"That's what you always say." Turning back to Herne Hill, Arnold asked, "Do you suppose you could stay for a few days? If I'm going to run harmonic convergence data through this program, I could use your help."

Herne was mellowed out completely. He said, "John and I have no place to hang our hat, we'd be honored to bunk in with you for a few days."

"You hear that, Vano? What do you think?"

"I think it would be very nice."

Just then, Sister Cecilia entered the room, carrying a basket of laundry.

Although he had never met her, Herne Hill recognized her immediately. "Hot damn! You must be Sister Cecilia! At last we meet!"

Since Sister had never seen Herne before, she was

confused, even as he began pumping her hand vigorously. "I've heard a lot about you, Little Lady, especially those glorious tits of yours!"

Sister recoiled, clutching a stack of folded tee shirts against her chest. She turned to Vano for solace, "Vano, listen how this man is speaking to me!"

"This is Herne Hill, Sister. He means no harm; it's just his manner of speaking."

Hill continued to address her: "I have a mental image of your body burned into my brain. It couldn't be more permanent if it was put there by a branding iron. The first time I heard your tits described, I damn near had to leave the room so as to take a few off."

"Vano, can't you do something?"

"He already has," Herne informed her. "His inspired description of your torso will cause a thousand wet dreams, or I'll eat my Harley buckle."

Sister began to dab at her moist eyes with Arnold's Kleenex. "Vano, did you tell about that night?"

Vano was deep, deep in, but he remembered. "I'm pretty sure the answer is yes."

"You told about that night!"

"It's true," he had to admit. "They wanted to hear about my first experience in deep *hooommm*."

She turned to Herne Hill for solace: "How could he do such a thing?"

"Think nothing of it, Little Lady. In the puzzle house, they hold nothing sacred. They drag everything right out of you."

"Is this true, Vano?"

"I believe it to be true."

"They scrape out your innermost secrets," Hill added, "And then try to convince you it's all for your own good. Vano had no choice, believe me."

Robin interrupted to say, "Let me make a suggestion. If Herne wants a better look at Sister's boobs, he'll just have to get up early and shower with her. The same as everybody else."

"I ought to be able to commit to that," said Herne. "Tell me what time the showering commences."

"About 7:30," said Robin.

"I'll be there," said Hill.

Vano was patting Sister Cecilia on the shoulder. "Do you feel better now?"

"Yes, I do." said Sister. "Thank you, Robin." She dabbed her eyes again before blowing her nose. "I don't mean to be a pill," she explained, "It's just hard being one of the boys sometimes."

Arnold said, "I have another suggestion. Since you're both musicians, why not play something together?"

"That's a wonderful idea," said Sister Cecilia. She took her trombone from the case while Herne moistened the mouthpiece of his french horn. The smell wasn't lost on John. "Llllllllll," he said.

The two of them played three hymns together, the last of which was *When the Roll is Called up Yonder*. They cobbled their separate styles together surprisingly well. Their encore was a rousing brass arrangement of *Dueling Banjos*.

*

It wasn't until a couple of days later that Herne got his invitation to interview with President Rose. He invited Vano to come with him.

"I think I would enjoy coming with you," said Vano.

As they were passing the main desk, Mrs. Kuetemeyer asked Herne if he could really play the French horn.

"You damn straight." To demonstrate, he blew a few bars of the Marlboro Man theme.

"Go ahead, then," said Mrs. Kuetemeyer.

Herne Hill had his motorcycle parked at the curb, an imposing blue and white Harley-Davidson *Electra-Glide*. "A little of my startup money is invested right here," he told Vano. "When the cash starts rolling in, I'm going to have a stereo and a miniature TV installed in this panel here."

"That sounds real nice, Herne."

Vano climbed aboard behind John, who was getting in place behind Herne. Owing to these cramped conditions, John's unruly thatch of brown hair was nearly flush with the tip of Vano's nose. Vano could see several tiny, pale insects maneuvering along the scalp.

They whisked away to the administration building on the huge, sleek Harley. Mrs. Askew showed them inside, where the threesome stood in front of Reggie Rose's desk. Herne Hill introduced himself first, then John, and finallly, Vano.

"Vano Lucas?" President Rose repeated the name. "Do I know you?"

From his ultra deep location, Vano was able to observe, "I don't think we've ever met."

"I'm sure your name sounds familiar, though." But Reggie was too unsettled by the appearance of Herne Hill to give the matter any further attention. He took a long look at Herne's leather vest and trousers, his bushy beard, his Harley accessories, his French horn, and his feral eyes. *God in Heaven,* Reggie thought to himself. *Is this to be the teacher?* When the president finally found his tongue, he asked, "Why is John here?"

"John is blind in this right eye, and 90 percent blind in the left one. He is deaf and dumb. And I do mean dumb, for his IQ is located somewhere in the range known as profoundly retarded. He's also emotionally disturbed. I usually take him wherever I go; it wouldn't be safe to leave him alone and unattended."

John said, "Lllllll."

"I can see your point," said Reggie Rose, "But what does he *do*?"

"I've taken John on as my business associate," Herne explained. "He doesn't have to do anything except sit where customers can look at him. He has a certain mystical quality which is good for business. In fact, if you take a close look at this eye here, you'll see how it looks like a miniature crystal ball." He was pointing to John's cloudy right eye.

"I see," murmured the president, fearing he was firm in the middle of a terrible mistake.

There was at this point in the conversation a protracted lull. Vano was in so deep that he could view this meeting along the far edge of the horizon. Taking advantage of the lull, Vano said to President Rose, "I'm a student here. I'm a friend of Herne's. If you prefer, I can leave."

Reggie wasn't sure how to respond. His mood was essentially upbeat, because Bertie Kerfoot was visiting her sister in Palm Springs.

It turned out not to matter. Herne Hill took up his French horn and said, "For my first number, I'd like to play *The Wayward Wind*, an old hit from the fifties by Gogi Grant." He proceeded to play the number without a single mistake.

Reggie brightened. "That's very good," he had to admit. Mrs. Askew appeared briefly from her own work area, but long enough to close the door.

"Thank you," said Herne Hill. "The French horn repertoire is rather limited, as I'm sure you know. But *The Theme from Robin Hood* is always a favorite. That will be my next number." This second number was so flawless in its appointment that Reggie was truly impressed.

"My final selection is one I've been working on lately. It's the theme from *Dallas*. Here goes." The theme from *Dallas* was even more inspiring than the first two offerings.

With a rush of enthusiasm, Reggie Rose jumped to his feet. He came out from behind his desk and began pumping Herne Hill's right hand. "Egad, you can play that horn! I'm so glad I didn't judge you based on my first impression. The job is yours!"

Vano, Herne, and John returned to the dorm. Herne announced to Robin and Arnold, "Buddy boys, I am in. I am now a member of the faculty."

Robin gave him a high five and a cold beer. Hill said, "When you're hot, you're hot! If you boys are ever lookin' for a stone cold *A*, you just sign yourselves up for Astrology 101."

Then Herne broke open a large box of individually-wrapped Twinkies. He and Robin put their feet up. Arnold Beeker might have participated in the giddiness of this euphoric moment, had it not been for his immediate computer agenda. "Please sit down," he said to Vano. "I have to show you this printout."

"Lllllllll," said John, as he maneuvered his way to the chair in front of the computer. Arnold interrupted himself long enough to boot up *Guns 'n' Martians*. John proceeded to press keys in a frenzy until he heard a repetitive beeping sound, at which time he began to giggle out of control.

Arnold returned to the printout, which he was

reviewing in a speed-reading kind of pattern, a foot or so at a time. He was rapidly tearing away sections of paper, then allowing them to drop to the floor. "Just a minute, just a minute," he said, in a voice tight with urgency. Finally, he found a very small section of the printout, which he tore free.

"This is it," declared Arnold. "Take a look at this."
Vano looked at the printing on the paper:

37.454N X 122.271N 0515GMT

But after reading it several times, he could only say, "This is very nice, Arnold."
"Don't you know what it means?"
"No, I don't."
"This is the read-out! This is the one!"
When Vano still drew a blank, Arnold explained, "This is it! This is the culmination! This read-out pinpoints exact time and place!"
"I see."
Nearly breathless though he was, Arnold couldn't help underscoring, "This is the perfect set of conditions we talked about for entering ultimate hoom!"
"Are you sure?"
"As sure as I can be. We have a date, which is today's, and we have a time, 9:15 P.M. our time. I've been able to identify the precise location as Alta Plaza Park in San Francisco."
After a few seconds Vano said, "I think it's very nice, Arnold. You deserve a lot of credit for working so hard."
"Thank you, but this is so totally cosmic it truly humbles me, Vano. I just kept putting the data in, folds in the earth superimposed on patterns of harmonic

convergence. Tell him what you said, Herne."

Herne Hill made his reply with four ounces of beer in his mouth, along with the better part of a Twinkie: "What I said to him was, garbage in, garbage out. You get the goods, you get the answer you need. It was bound to happen."

"Do you see, Vano?"

"No, Arnold, to be honest, I don't."

First Arnold made a face, and then he held up his watch so Vano could see. "We don't have time to go into it now, it's past two o'clock. If we're going to get there on time, we need to get started."

Vano receded a little deeper down. "Are we going to San Francisco today?"

"We *have* to," Arnold insisted. "There's no other choice. We may be on the threshold of the greatest discovery since fire or the wheel! We can't look the opportunity in the face and turn the other way."

Vano formed the question, "How will we get there?"

"We have your Lincoln. Sister Cecilia says it's no problem if we want to use it."

The Twinkie finished and his beer can empty, Herne Hill was on his feet. He did a little gapping and stretching, then embarked on a series of long and loud belches. He was combing his beard with his fingers so as to distribute crumbs on Robin's bedspread. He said to Vano, "To go or not to go, *Amigo*; that is the question."

"It would be very nice to go to San Francisco," said Vano.

"Give me a few minutes to round up Rita," said Herne. "She wouldn't miss this trip for anything." He was referring to Rita Lieberman, with whom he had succeeded in establishing a carnal relationship during his few days on campus. "When I return, I'll be ready."

After a few moments of pondering, Vano said, "Chaplain Johansen needs to go to Salinas. Can we offer him a ride?"

"Salinas is right on the way," Hill noted. "The more the merrier is how I look at it." Then he left.

Arnold began immediate preparation for the journey by doubling up on the adhesive tape which reinforced his glasses. He started to pack his Alpine backpack. "I wouldn't have all this stuff if it wasn't for the spelunking club," he reminded Vano. In went some maps, a compass, his calculator, fresh batteries, the crucial pages of printout, the Arguelles book, Revuelto's manuscript, several number two pencils, and a translucent yellow plastic pencil sharpener from Sav-On.

From deeper down, Vano was watching him. "You'd better get your stuff ready," Arnold told him.

"I don't have any stuff. I think I'm as ready as I'll ever be."

Sister Cecilia entered the room, carrying the laundry basket. She began folding towels and stacking them on Vano's dresser.

"Sister, we're going to San Francisco. Would you like to come with us?"

"Thank you, Vano, but I think I have too much to do."

Vano wondered if he should try and explain how this was more than a trip to the store. If he passed over into *ultimate hooommm*, then he would never see her again.

"I have two more loads of laundry and lots of ironing," Sister continued. "I'm glad you're back, though; I need to talk to you."

John giggled madly at a beeping laser just before Sister said, "I don't think it's a good idea for me to stay here any longer. I think it's time I moved out."

Vano pointed out, "All the guys think highly of you, Sister."

"I know. They've all been so accepting and supportive. This is a wonderful place for you and your friends, but I can't fit in, not over the long haul. I'm not discouraged though, because the Lord has made known His will to me. He has led me to understand what to do with myself."

"What's that?" asked Vano.

"If it's all right with you, I'd like to keep on living at the condo. There's so much upkeep to do, even when I'm there by myself. Did you know that furnace filters have to be changed every month?"

"Even if the furnace isn't running?"

"I'm pretty sure."

"I didn't know that," Vano admitted.

"Besides that, there's the Salvation Army band. You know how much the band means to me."

"I know how much the band means to you. I think it would be real nice if you stayed on at the condo."

Herne Hill appeared in the doorway to announce that Rita was waiting in the car. Spying Sister, he made a request: "Little Lady, if we're going to San Fran, I'm going to have to leave John in your care. I hope you don't mind. He's getting such a kick out of the computer, I doubt if he'll need much attention."

"Your father didn't have a current will, Vano. He was changing the terms of it after the accident. His estate is going to be in probate for a long time, I'm afraid."

Herne said, "I might as well warn you, John has a habit of beating his meat. If he gets that action going, I advise you to more or less ignore it. I think he can tell if he's being watched, just don't ask me how."

"With all his business interests and the investment

portfolio, there's going to be a lot of red tape to unravel in the months ahead. I'm sure it would keep me busy for a long time. It would take several hours a day just to write the necessary letters."

Vano agreed. "I can see your point."

Herne said, "It makes some people uptight when he does it in public, but I say hey, what the hell? Live and let live. He's blind, he can't talk, and he's retarded. He deserves a little pleasure out of life, am I right?"

"Vano, what I'm trying to say is, I'd like to be the executor of your father's estate. Of course, I would need your permission."

"I think it sounds real nice, Sister. It sounds real logical to me."

Herne Hill brought his agenda to a conclusion by adding, "Course, you being a woman and all, you could probably send John straight to the moon if you was to get in a few strokes of your own. Let's just leave that part optional, though."

"For several years, I've been doing a lot of your father's basic transactions like the checking account, the savings account, the certificates of deposit, the municipal bonds, and the IRA's. I could send you the same funds you're getting now, pay your school bills, and so on. In a little while, we might not even notice that your father is gone."

"We might not even notice," murmured Vano.

Arnold Beeker spoke up for the first time to say, "Vano, I've got to be completely honest with you. Even though this is totally cosmic, and even though it may be the most important event since the discovery of fire, I have a few reservations. I've got to be honest."

Vano understood what he was talking about. For the second time, he wondered if he should share with Sister how this might be a permanent farewell. But Herne Hill interrupted his train of thought: "Boys, this is no time for wet feet. The time has come."

On the way to the car, Arnold tried to define the manner of his trepidation: "This is a bittersweet situation. It's sweet because I figured out how to load the right data, which may lead to a great discovery. It's bitter because if it works, it means I won't be seeing you any more."

"I understand."

"If you go into ultimate hoom, you'll be in particle existence. I won't be seeing you any more. I'll have myself to blame, because I just had to feed that data."

Vano's delay was a short one. "You did what you do best, Arnold. It's something to be proud of. Besides, nothing in the universe is permanent."

"I suppose you think that's a good answer. I suppose you think that's some kind of consolation. I think this whole thing is mind-blowing."

Vano said, "Most likely, that's what it is exactly."

"Are you some kind of prophet or something? Is that why you were chosen?"

"Of course not."

"But you were *chosen*."

"I was only chosen because I had preliminary experience in *hooommm*. There were others before me and there will be others again. It's inevitable in a universe of waves and particles."

"I suppose you think that's a good answer."

Herne slid in behind the wheel, with Rita beside him. Arnold rode on the passenger's side in front. Vano and the chaplain sat in the back seat on either side of Rita's Aztec statue. They purred north at high speed on the Pacific Coast Highway. The sun was playing hide and seek among the clouds. Vano shimmered in the merger of earth and sky and sea.

The chaplain and Vano conducted an over-the-statue conversation. The chaplain said, "Arnold Beeker tells me you were once a great pitcher."

"I think that's true," Vano replied. It was only a few months ago, yet it seemed so distant, practically like a different lifetime.

"You seem so contemplative to be an athlete. I hope that's not an offensive remark."

"It's not offensive. Taking offense is not a part of *hooommm*."

Chaplain Johansen told Vano that Coach Radulski wasn't on the staff any more. He was in a rehab center. "Did you know that?"

"No," said Vano. "I didn't know. What I do know is that Coach Radulski was depending on me to cover the Entrada baseball team with fame and glory. He thought the program would become the recipient of millions of dollars in gate receipts and television revenue."

"But you mustn't feel guilty, my son. The coach had a serious problem with alcohol abuse long before he met you."

"I don't feel guilty," Vano replied. "Guilt is not a part of *hooommm*."

Chaplain Johansen tilted the angle of the statue so he could make eye contact. "Just thinking out loud, but it may turn out that your presence may still be of major economic benefit to Entrada."

Vano was in too deep to process this change of direction quickly. "I don't think I understand."

"What I mean to say is that Wilfong Weingrad was inclined to give us this huge endowment after he read a memo I wrote. That memo was based on the material you gave me about particle dust intelligence floating through the heavens."

Hooommm. "I see."

The chaplain continued, "I thought you should know, because if the college does receive the gift, most of the credit will belong to you."

The pause lingered before Vano answered politely, "The truth is, what I know about particle existence comes from the particle people. Not from me."

When they reached rural Salinas, they needed to stop at nearly every intersection to check directions. Chaplain Johansen referred to his map, while Arnold looked his calculations over. Since Rita Lieberman was sliding her hand inside his pants at every stop, Herne Hill had no objection to the frequency of these delays.

Their combined reconnaisance proved successful. The sun was low by the time they pulled to a stop in front of Weingrad's remarkable mailbox, perched next to the lonely stretch of blacktop. "This is a crusader," observed Chaplain Johansen. "Weingrad's mailbox is a statue of a crusader."

Herne Hill couldn't help but admire the statue's rigid attire. "Hot damn, look at the chain-mail. I could see myself wearing these duds on the Harley. I wonder if the armor comes off."

Chaplain Johansen felt a knot of tension forming in his stomach as he looked closely at the security system which sealed Weingrad's premises from the rest of the world. Near the road was a chain-link fence, 12 feet high, with spirals of barbed wire bristling along the top. A large, painted sign was posted on the fence:

WARNING: ELECTRIFIED FENCE. THESE PREMISES GUARDED BY KILLER ATTACK DOBERMANS

Despite these daunting admonitions, however, the

gate was open. Herne shot the car up the long lane, spinning gravel.

The chaplain got out of the car, but owing to his escalating case of nerves, he spoke briefly with Herne: "This shouldn't take too long. You'll be right here when I'm finished?"

Before he could answer, Herne had to lift his head from beneath Rita's skirt. "We'll be right here, Bro." Droplets of drool bobbed on his beard.

The chaplain didn't notice these logistics, so absorbed was he by the tension of his imminent mission. He rubbed his hands together several times. "Thank you," he finally said.

"We'll even have the motor runnin'."

Arnold Beeker put in his two cents: "I hope so. It's very important to get to Alta Plaza on time."

Chaplain Johansen paced uneasily on the front porch after ringing the bell. His uneasiness increased when Grizelda opened the door to greet him. She was a large, barrel-chested woman with solid forearms. Her breath smelled of whiskey. "You haff come for seekink Wilfong?" she asked.

Chaplain Johansen confirmed it, but he asked her if she could give him a little information about the potential benefactor.

"Wilfong hass cuckoo," said Grizelda.

"Wilfong hass cuckoo?"

"Don't dare to make spordt mitt Grizelda!" warned the formidable housekeeper. She grinded her right fist into her left palm. The chaplain stared at the huge fists. She could probably pound him into the ground like a tent stake.

The house was poorly lit. Grizelda led Johansen to the basement where Wilfong was playing with his electric trains. The very elaborate train set treatments were precise in much detail. Wilfong Weingrad operated the transformer with unrestrained glee. He wore a striped engineer's cap while shouting "Woo woo!" every now and again. The trains zoomed around the tracks.

After Grizelda informed him it was Chaplain Johansen from the college, he took his guest upstairs to the study.

It was in this room that Johansen saw the 32 cuckoo clocks on the wall. *So this was what Grizelda meant.* Without thinking, the chaplain blurted out, "You hass cuckoo."

"You hass cuckoo?" asked Weingrad.

Chaplain Johansen felt like a fool. He got red in the face. In a panic, he tried to think of some manner of explanation for his remark, but he was speechless.

It didn't matter in the least. Weingrad was sitting at his desk and getting out his Bible. He was wrapping the wire frames of his glasses around his ears. The pink scalp glistened through the few white hairs.

Wilfong laid it on the line: "These are the Last Days, so I hope you're prepared for the Apocalypse! The Beast is all around us. The Lord is coming in his fury to smite the enemy with His terrible, swift sword! Do you have the fear o' the Lord in you? Does your college have the fear o' the Lord?"

Still very nervous, Chaplain Johansen tiptoed in the direction of some cautious speculation: "I would say that's a difficult question. First, we would have to examine what we mean by fear."

His tentative preamble was as irrelevant to Weingrad as the relative humidity in Chula Vista. "I will give the 25 million dollars if you have the fear o' the Lord! Having said this, Weingrad proceeded to read from Revelation the description of the Lord coming from Heaven as a warrior on a white horse. So moved was he by this battle imagery, he embellished with a few details of his own device: "He will be armed to the teeth! He will have a sword and a double-bladed ax and he will be outfitted with shining armor. It won't be ordinary armor either, but chain-mail! There will be steel mesh on his terrible, swift fists!" At this point, red in the face and short of breath, he had to pause.

Chaplain Johansen had concluded by now that Wilfong was unbalanced, but this knowledge did nothing to allay his discomfort. At this moment, the 32 cuckoo clocks began going off. It was a startling, nerve-wracking cacaphony which provoked Johansen to jump to his feet. For his part, Weingrad was merely annoyed. He jerked out his hearing aide and threw it on top of his desk.

He was now deaf as a stone. Hearing nothing, he shuffled across the room. "Goddamit, Woman! You're not to wind these clocks! How many times have you been told?" The clocks were slightly out of sync, which meant they would be sounding for quite some time. On the other side of the room, Wilfong punched a button on a control panel to shut off the clocks. By accident, he punched the wrong button, which activated the warning siren which was part of the security system.

To the chaplain, it sounded as if a squad car had just entered the room. His pulse increased to 205, and he broke a sweat. The clocks cuckooed while the siren screamed. But hearing not a sound, Weingrad returned to his seat behind the desk; he resumed the reading from Revelation.

Johansen didn't know how much more he could stand. While there were shrill cuckoo clocks and a wailing siren, Weingrad was reading from the scriptures and moving his lips. Then two large dobermans came racing into the room, snarling and baring their fangs. They stood four feet from Johansen while curling back their lips and growling their menacing growls.

    In great fear, Chaplain Johansen jumped up onto his chair. He covered most of his face with his hands. Weingrad was still absorbed in the text. Grizelda came charging in. "Shut up the noiss!! Mein Gott, shut up the noiss!"

    Weingrad was aware of nothing save his chapter and verse, but the chaplain was in such terror he feared his sphincters were about to dysfunction. The dobermans seemed to irritate Grizelda more than the clocks or the siren. She doubled her fist and socked the larger of the two dogs on the jaw. The dog tumbled over and began to whimper, but the other one held its position while maintaining its snarl.

    Grizelda crossed the room in long, impatient strides. She punched the right buttons, so that everything was suddenly silent. Only Weingrad's voice was audible. The upright doberman still had its teeth bared. Drenched in his own sweat, Chaplain Johansen wondered if his pants were peed.

    Then Weingrad, having finished the passage, looked up from his Bible to see Chaplain Johansen standing on his chair and cowering in utter terror. This, Weingrad presumed, was Johansen's reaction to the passages of scripture vis-a-vis the End Times. Wilfong pounded his measly fist into his measly palm. "By Jove, Grizelda, would you look at this? This boy has the fear o' the Lord in him or I'll eat my hat!"

    Grizelda was leaving the room. "Cuckoo!" she exclaimed. "All hass cuckoo!"

    When the chaplain returned to the car, he was contending with the full range of stress-associated symptoms. Sweaty palms, dry mouth, increased pulse rate, elevated blood pressure, flushing, and shortness of breath. In response to the curiosity of his colleagues, he could give only the briefest summary of his bizarre encounter. He was much too shaken to review in detail. To calm his nerves he tried some deep breathing and a short pull on Herne's bottle of Wild Turkey. They were clear to Santa Cruz, though, before he recovered a comfortable level of equilibrium.

Arnold Beeker was afraid they might be running late, so he navigated Herne and the Lincoln into the Bay Area by way of Interstate 280.

As soon as they arrived at Alta Plaza Park, Vano had instant recognition. This place was the dream. Ancient but urban, the huge park formed a mountainous, terraced pyramid. The wind began to blow.

"Arnold, this is it."

"I can read maps, Vano; Alta Plaza isn't hard to find."

"That's not what I mean. I mean this is *it*."

"This is what?"

"This is my dream. This is the pyramid. This is the place."

"Oh my god, Vano, oh my god. Did we need another sign?"

They ascended the stairs, but slowly. There were many flights. Arnold urged them on. "Time is of the essence!" he implored.

On each level, the stronger wind seemed to blow colder. To complicate matters, Rita Lieberman struggled with her Aztec statue, stopping frequently to shift its weight from one shoulder to the other. Herne Hill helped out by carrying it a flight or two, but then he handed it back. "Piss on this," he said. "Why didn't you leave the damn thing back in the car?"

"Oh sure, just leave it where anybody might steal it. You got any idea what this statue is worth?"

Vano wondered if he should remind Rita that the

statue was most likely manufactured in San Diego or South Korea. Maybe she forgot that Revuelto had two more of them in the closet? But he had no voice with which to speak; he was overwhelmed by the orange sea which lapped the sky and the inner chamber vibrations which were shaking the firmament.

"It's cold up here," observed Chaplain Johansen. He buttoned the top button of his cardigan sweater to shield against the wind.

"It's colder 'n a witch's tit," Rita agreed. "This is nuts, why did I even come here?"

Cold wind or no, when they reached the top they gained the breathtaking view of the Bay Area after dark. By looking north, Vano could see beyond the vista of city lights clear to Sausalito. Alan Watts was dead, but was his houseboat still moored there? To the east, across San Francisco Bay, he could see the twinkling galaxy of Oakland. Which of those lights, he wondered, burned atop Oakland Alameda County Stadium?"

It was a confluence of physical and psychic forces which shook him to the depths of his soul. It was exhilarating. Like those few other times, he felt the world wobble on its axis. He stood at the threshold of *Ultimate Hooommm*, no doubt about it. Would it be a matter of minutes, or merely seconds?

Arnold could see the body language. "Are you scared?" he asked Vano.

"No," replied Vano. The lights were going dim. "Fear is not a part of *hooommm*."

"You don't have to yell," replied his friend. For Arnold and the others, there were no roaring chambers, no oceanic gongs timbring from the nether trail of the solar system. No shaking firmament. Nothing at all, in fact, to modify the ordinary patterns of their senses.

"What did you say?" asked Vano in a loud voice, as he assumed the lotus position in the grass.

"I was saying it's too bad Mary Thorne couldn't be here."

"Mary will be fine."

"Let's don't talk about that babe," said Herne Hill. "I don't think I could stand it."

Rita Lieberman asked Arnold, "What did you say about Mary Thorne?"

But Herne didn't give him a chance to answer. "Do me a favor, Rita; stroke me off whilst I try to visualize her in the altogether. Talk about your harmonic convergence! Talk about your ultimate hoom!"

"Why you low-life sonofabitch! If I had my nail file with me I'd cut your balls off and hand you a pair of earrings. You bastard." Rita swung her statue savagely at him, but Herne ducked.

Thrown off balance by her near-miss, Rita lost her grip. The base of the statue clipped Vano right above his left ear. He toppled over like a stone. A millisecond of bursting stars and shimmering seas preceded his state of profound unconsciousness.

Ultimate hooommm would have to wait.

Epilogue

The decision by the Oakland A's to pitch Vano Lucas on opening day the following April, created a crowd control problem of drastic proportions. Team officials bulged Alameda County Stadium at the seams by putting 12,000 standing-room-only tickets on sale two hours before game time. Even with this provision, the multitudes who swarmed the pavement outside engaged in a frenzy of bartering and ticket scalping.

Vano loosened in the bullpen 30 minutes before the game, throwing easily at first, then unleashing his 100 mph plus fastballs into the mitt of Jerome Neal, the bullpen catcher. Each pitch impacted like a cherry bomb explosion. *Crack*! Neal's good judgment compelled him to wear full protective gear during this prelude, including nut cup. Especially nut cup.

Spectators by the hundreds crowded as close as

possible to view this warm-up action, straining the deployment of stadium ushers. The fans oohed and aahed at Vano's velocity, and they shouted his name.

Stuck among the crowd, one who hollered was Arnold Beeker. "I have to talk to you!" he kept yelling. Somehow, he succeeded in getting Vano's attention.

Vano waved, then yelled back, "In a minute!" He had a full sweat. His arm felt loose and live; he was pumped. He activated a cheer which swept through the stadium when he walked from the bullpen to the dugout, his Oakland windbreaker draped over his right shoulder. Ignoring the crowd of autograph seekers near the dugout, he was able to gain access for Arnold by means of the field gate near the dugout.

"I have to talk to you," said Arnold, repeating himself.

"Come on, we'll go into the clubhouse. With this sweat, I want to wear an undershirt."

Arnold tripped on the dugout steps, but managed to recover his balance in time to avoid falling. "Gosh," he said, "That's Ricky Henderson."

There were only a few people in the clubhouse. Some of the players, finished with batting practice, were changing uniform shirts. Dave Stewart was having an ankle taped.

"It's been impossible to get in touch with you. Now that you're a superstar, nobody can talk to you."

"I know what you mean. Even Sister has to leave messages with the GM's secretary. Spring training's over now, though; we can get together." Vano took his shirt off. He began sorting through a stack of three-quarter sleeve undershirts placed on the table by the equipment manager.

"Weingrad gave Entrada the 25 million," said Arnold.

"That's what I heard. The same as my signing bonus; some coincidence, huh?"

"That's what Chaplain Johansen calls it, but after what we went through, I'm not sure if I believe in coincidence." But Arnold knew this chit-chat wouldn't do; his window of opportunity here was brief. He needed to get right to the point.

"Vano, what's going to become of hoom?"

Using a towel to mop the moisture from his torso, Vano simply gave a shrug.

"And what about particle existence?" persisted Arnold. "What about that? I know you have this wonderful baseball career now and lots of money, but can you just walk away from something as cosmic as that was? Can you just pretend like it never happened?"

Vano shrugged again. "I don't know what else to do."

"Please."

"Arnold, that's the past. You're talking about the past, but now it's time for me to move on."

"It can't be the past, though. You said yourself there's no past in hoom because it's timeless."

Smiling, Vano patted his earnest friend on the shoulder. "Take it easy, Arnold. Nothing is forever. The second coma brought me back to my senses. You're talking about the *old* me."

"No, I'm not talking about the *old* you, I'm talking about the *real* you."

Vano found the shirt he was seeking, one with extra-absorbent sleeves. He pulled it on over his head. "I don't follow you."

"Vano, I have this theory."

Vano found himself losing patience. He laughed anyway. "You'll never run out of theories, it's what you do."

"But this is different. Really. Before you turn your back on hoom completely, you have to hear me out. Please." Arnold put his glasses on, as if to sharpen his verbal focus.

"Okay, okay, you can tell me the theory, but there's only a few minutes. Don't forget, this is my big day."

"I know. I'm really sorry. If there was any other way. But here's the theory: hoom was just you. It was a chance for the real you to come to the surface. It didn't have anything to do with particle people, or waves, or other dimensions. It didn't have anything to do with the Federation, or harmonic convergence. It was just a set of conditions which gave you the freedom to be yourself."

Vano didn't answer. He was listening to Arnold's observations while putting on the Oakland A's uniform shirt with the green and gold insignia. The large number 50.

Arnold got to the core: "Alan Watts was your father, even though he never married your mother. You had two contemplative, mystical parents. That's your real genetic code. That's the person you really are deep down inside, but as a superstar jock, that person never had a chance to surface."

Jerome Neal stuck his head in the doorway to tell Vano, "Three minutes, Kid, and they're going to start blowing the Star Spangled Banner. Still feel okay?"

"Yeah, I feel great. I'm ready."

As soon as Neal's face disappeared, Arnold continued. "You just never got to be you. You may never get to be you again--there just won't be room for it in the world of big shots and fame and all that stuff."

Vano looked at him before he answered. Impatience or no, he liked Arnold. Arnold was his friend. He finally said, "Arnold, it's time for me to pitch."

"The public will never stand for the real Vano Lucas. The public won't stand for anything that's real. Hoom was all about the freedom to be who you are. It wasn't supernatural at all, but it still had a terrific meaning. You see what I'm saying, don't you?"

They were walking toward the dugout. Vano threw his arm over his friend's bony shoulder. "It's a real interesting theory, Arnold. After the game, maybe I'll have some time to think about it."

They stood on the top step of the dugout while Jose Canseco, Ricky Henderson, Mark McGuire, and the other celebrities were introduced by the public address announcer. Each player jogged to the first base line as his name was called, to join the row formed by his teammates. Each time a player was introduced, there was a blast of sound as the huge crowd cheered.

Overwhelmed in this setting, Arnold Beeker was speechless. Vano was staring at a beautiful blond sitting in a box seat at eye level. She was wearing a short pink skirt but no underwear. She sat with her legs parted and a smile on her face. She was looking straight at him. Vano didn't know who she was, but he smiled back and mouthed the words, "Thank you."

"You'll forget all about ultimate hoom, won't you?" Arnold was yelling above the din.

"This is ultimate hoom," Vano yelled back. The grin on his face spread nearly from ear to ear.

"It'll be like it never happened, won't it?"

The public address announcer was beginning Vano's introduction with the words, "Number 50." The noise began to swell. Just before he left to join his line of teammates, Vano hollered to Arnold once again, "This *is* ultimate hoom!"

Then he turned away. He jogged toward first base,

rotating his draped right shoulder to keep it warm and loose. The roar of the crowd was deafening.

Also by James Bennett:

I Can Hear the Mourning Dove
(Houghton -Mifflin 1990):
"One of the ten best young adult novels of 1990."-*Publishers Weekly*

An American Library Association **Best Books for Young Adults** selection

Dakota Dream (Scholastic 1994):
"Mr. Bennett has crafted a unique and stunning coming-of-age novel."
-*Joni Richards Bodart*

"Bennett's astute novel demonstrates enormous sensitivity."-*Publishers Weekly*

The Squared Circle (Scholastic 1995):
"A vivid, heartrending story of a top athlete struggling to leave the glory road and find his own path." -*Kirkus, Books of Note*

"The finest...novel of 1995. It is a masterpiece: scene after scene sears the brain."
-*V.O.Y.A.*

"This is a sobering read that should be thrust into the hands of any high school students who are contemplating playing revenue-producing sports at major universities."
-*School Library Journal*